Claire was sending an email on her phone to a vendor to begin discussing wine options for an upcoming fundraising event. As she hit send, she noticed that Danielle had uncharacteristically set her phone down on the table and was staring across the crowded restaurant.

Though Claire glanced in that direction, she didn't see anything out of the ordinary.

Then she heard his laugh.

Every nerve cell in her body tensed.

And a memory from twenty plus years ago was awakened.

"Mom?" Danielle whispered. "It's him."

"It's who?" She whispered back, but her eyes were glued to the handsome man in the white shirt and black slacks three tables over. He sported two-day old stubble on his face and his hair was still thick and dark.

Tall, dark, and handsome.

That's always how she'd thought of Grayson Moore. Now he was even more handsome with twenty years of maturity on him. If she hadn't heard his laugh, she probably wouldn't even have noticed him. Well, she would have noticed him, but she wouldn't have recognized him.

"It's Grayson," Danielle said. "My psych teacher."

No. Way.

"Come on," Danielle said. "I'll introduce you."

Grayson was with another man, a student perhaps? Or a

younger colleague? "No," she said, but Danielle was already standing up and walking toward his table.

Claire was in full panic mode.

This couldn't happen. Not like this. She got up and walked the other way. Toward the restroom. She needed a second. Just one second.

Claire Worthington didn't panic.

LOVE AGAIN

LOVE AGAIN

THE WORTHINGTONS

KATHRYN KALEIGH

To learn more about Kathryn Kaleigh, visit

www.kathrynkaleigh.com

Kathryn Kaleigh

*C*laire Worthington believed that life moved in only one direction. Forward.

"Mom!" Danielle said excitedly as she approached Claire down the wide UCLA hallway. "My psychology class is so lit. The instructor is on fire."

Claire gathered up her iPhone and iPad, drew her handbag over her shoulders. She'd been waiting for two hours for her daughter's classes to end. "So… you like it?" Claire asked for clarification.

Danielle grinned. "It's gonna be awesome."

"That's great," she said. Claire glanced at her watch. She had just enough time to get Danielle to her counseling session at Resolutions Treatment Center, then they could have a quick lunch before Claire's meeting with a new artist coming in at two o'clock.

They walked together down the hall at UCLA, dodging students hurrying to their next class, most of them looking down at their phones.

"He runs the Psychology Clinic, so he's gonna let us observe some sessions. Can you believe it? It's my first semester and I already get to observe."

"That's great, honey," Claire said. Ever since Danielle began mental health treatment last winter, she'd been dead-set on studying psychology. She'd been so disappointed that her hospitalization had caused her to drop out of her advanced classes in the spring, that Claire had pulled some strings and gotten her into summer classes at the university at the last minute.

Scheduling had been an utter nightmare ever since. Spring had been a process of Danielle finishing up high school in Ft. Worth and moving to Los Angeles. Fortunately, Claire already had a house in L.A. Considering everything that had happened in the last few months, the move had gone smoothly.

Since Claire had to attend mental health counseling with Danielle twice a week, Claire drove her to class those days.

"Grayson is even going to have an art therapist come talk to us so we can see what that's like."

Claire stopped and gazed at her daughter, causing the other students to flow around them.

"Mom, what?" Danielle had that panicky *Please don't let the other students find out I have parents* look on her face. "Come on."

Claire followed, but her brain remained frozen. The art therapy part was interesting and Claire wanted to hear more about it. Later.

Something else entirely had her attention, however, at the moment.

Grayson.

A name that was becoming more popular with babies born today, but quite unusual during Claire's generation. She knew because she'd looked it up.

Did she dare ask?

She had to know. "What's his last name?" she asked, holding her breath.

Danielle shifted her backpack and smiled as she checked an incoming text. "I don't know," she said, keeping her eyes on her phone. "Can we skip therapy today?"

"No," Claire said automatically, exhaling in frustration. Danielle asked the same question nearly every day. Today, however, her daughter was particularly glowing. The psychologist had warned her that Danielle would have fleeting moments of happiness. But that had been months ago. Surely at some point she no longer had to worry when her daughter was happy.

"What did he look like?" She asked.

"Grayson?"

"Yes. Shouldn't you call him Dr. or Mr. or something?"

Danielle rolled her eyes. "It's not the south, Mom. It's L.A." Then she stopped texting and looked up at her mother. "Cute," she said. "About Daddy's size. Your age maybe. I don't know. Do you want me to find out if he's married?"

"Heavens no!" Claire said, feeling the flush on her cheeks.

"Why do you want to know?"

"I had a friend in high school named Grayson. But it couldn't possibly be the same guy."

Danielle shook her head and attached her gaze back to her phone. "No way. He wouldn't have been your type. This guy just retired from the Air Force."

Claire clasped a hand over her mouth to keep from gasping. Grayson Moore had been in the delayed entry program and entered the Air Force the day after graduation. He'd promised to write, but he hadn't. Not even once. Not one letter. Not one phone call. It was twenty years ago, so they hadn't had cell phones. Well, Claire had a cell phone, but Grayson didn't. Grayson hadn't had email either.

She sighed as she steered Danielle, whose attention was glued to her phone, her fingers flying over the screen, toward the car. Things would have been so much different if they'd simply had cell phones back then.

The name and the Air Force part matched up, but a psychology instructor? Claire tapped her fingers on the steering wheel as she waited for traffic to move.

That didn't fit. Not even a little.

DANIELLE'S THERAPY session was uneventful. Danielle seemed to be truly excited to be starting college. Her daughter had just gotten back from spending a week with her father Noah and his new wife. Claire and Noah had been divorced just over six months. Noah had gotten married the day after he and Claire had officially gotten divorced. Talk about not letting the ink dry.

But Claire was happy to have it over with. Now she didn't have to worry about the obligatory visits to Ft. Worth to be with her husband.

Claire had a house in L.A. and a growing business. She'd been growing her business for years, but her husband had no idea. He thought she was here sipping mimosas with her girlfriends.

Technically, she began to network before she even married Noah. By the time they were married, she was having business meetings several times a week. Throughout the early part of their marriage, Noah thought Claire was taking money from her father to supplement Noah's income. She never told him the truth. She'd been earning the money and never once touched her father's. Well, that didn't include the start-up money her father had given her, but Claire didn't count that since she'd paid it off in mere months.

After the session, she and Danielle drove back toward the university and had lunch at a trendy little restaurant set up in the middle of a greenhouse. Claire ordered a fried green tomato po'boy with avocados, and veggie bacon and Danielle ordered a shrimp po'boy. If the two of them had a favorite restaurant to go to together, it would have to be this one. It was called the York and Orleans and they both had favorite lunch items on the menu.

Claire was sending an email on her phone to a vendor to begin discussing wine options for an upcoming fundraising event. As she hit send, she noticed that Danielle had uncharacteristically set her phone down on the table and was staring across the crowded restaurant.

Though Claire glanced in that direction, she didn't see anything out of the ordinary.

Then she heard his laugh.

Every nerve cell in her body tensed.

And a memory from twenty plus years ago was awakened.

"Mom?" Danielle whispered. "It's him."

"It's who?" She whispered back, but her eyes were glued to the handsome man in the white shirt and black slacks three tables over. He sported two-day old stubble on his face and his hair was still thick and dark.

Tall, dark, and handsome.

That's always how she'd thought of Grayson Moore. Now he was even more handsome with twenty years of maturity on him. If she hadn't heard his laugh, she probably wouldn't even have noticed him. Well, she would have noticed him, but she wouldn't have recognized him.

"It's Grayson," Danielle said. "My psych teacher."

No. Way.

"Come on," Danielle said. "I'll introduce you."

Grayson was with another man, a student perhaps? Or a younger colleague? "No," she said, but Danielle was already standing up and walking toward his table.

Claire was in full panic mode.

This couldn't happen. Not like this. She got up and walked

the other way. Toward the restroom. She needed a second. Just one second.

Claire Worthington didn't panic.

GRAYSON MOORE RECOGNIZED the student who stood at his table. He rarely did, especially after only the first day, but this particular student had been especially enthusiastic and there had been something about her smile that had caught his attention.

"Hi," she said with that smile. "I'm sorry to interrupt, but I'm in your psychology class. From today."

"Sure," Grayson said. "How are you?"

"I'm good. I'm really excited about the class, but... I think my mom knows you. Or something." The student was frowning now and looking across the restaurant. "I was going to introduce you, but she... left."

"Your mother?" He looked past the girl, searching for someone who looked motherly.

"Yeah. We're having lunch," The girl stood next to his chair, searching the restaurant for her missing mother.

Grayson glanced at Bob, an applicant for a teaching position. Shrugged as though to say *this happens sometimes.*

Bob seemed unaffected. In fact, he used the distraction to finish off his sandwich.

"It's okay," Grayson said. "I can meet her next time."

He followed the girl's gaze toward the restroom and his eyes locked on the woman walking toward them. His dream woman.

Literally. The woman walking toward them had the same lithe movements as his high school sweetheart.

He knew, however, that it wasn't her. His high school sweetheart was blonde. And this woman was brunette. He looked more closely at the student with her red bow shaped lips. Then back at the woman walking toward them. He knew that smile. "It's Claire," he said.

"Yeah," Danielle said. "That's my mother." She jerked her head around to stare at Grayson. "Wait. How do you know her name?"

Grayson couldn't answer. His tongue was tied up in knots. The man who talked for a living couldn't put two syllables together in his head to save his own life at this moment.

Claire stood at his table now, next to her daughter, and Grayson knew why the student's smile had caught his attention. It was her mother's smile. The one he had known so well.

Twenty years ago.

His eyes strayed to her lips and his neurons traveled down a path he thought had long been severed from his brain.

"Grayson," Claire said. "It's good to see you. You've met my daughter, Danielle."

His brain chemistry was scrambled, but he found himself reflexively returning her smile. Claire may be brunette now, but she was still the girl he'd loved in high school. "It's good to see you, too, Claire. Where have you been?"

"I stepped into the lady's room," she said, her eyes wide with innocence.

Grayson didn't buy the innocence. She knew he wasn't being literal. But he let it go for now. When her daughter wasn't standing next to her, he'd ask again and this time he'd add the words *for the last twenty years* to his question.

"My daughter has been raving about your class since this morning."

"I try to make things interesting," he said, trying to ignore the ringing in his ears. He was trying to wrap his head around Claire having a daughter. They'd talked about having children. Claire had wanted two – a boy and a girl. Grayson had wanted four. Did she have other children? Now that his brain was thawing, so many questions were beginning to form.

If Claire had a child, she was married. Claire Beauchamp was nothing if not traditional. He glanced at her ring finger. No ring. Divorced then. There was a simple diamond on her index finger. And a small diamond on a silver chain around her neck and larger diamonds in her ears. She wore a red pencil skirt with a white jacket cropped to her waist. Black pumps with red bottoms graced her feet. A Gucci handbag hung across her shoulders. Grayson had no doubt that the things she wore at this moment cost more than a month's salary for him.

That was the Claire he knew. *Where did you go?*

He wanted to talk to her. Needed to talk to her.

CLAIRE DROPPED her daughter off at her friend's house and drove the thirty minutes to the gallery. She had plenty of time to get everything ready before the artist came in at 2:00. The fundraiser was in two weeks, so she had plenty of time. She had it down to a science.

She could only hope that the artist, Maine D'Court, had come through and had enough paintings ready to show. He'd promised her that he worked fast.

Claire wasn't sure that fast was necessarily a good thing in the art world, but it was probably like everything else. It wasn't the speed at which something was done, it was the perseverance.

Maine D'Court had come through. He had brought three paintings in addition to those he had promised.

Maine already had the paintings inside and set up for her look at when Claire got to the gallery.

She should have been elated. Could have been elated. Would have been elated.

If she hadn't just encountered the one man she had ever loved.

So, instead of elated, she was… edgy.

It was the only way she knew to describe the nerves tingling through her body.

She and Grayson had dated her sophomore and junior years in high school. He was one year older, so when he graduated, he had joined the Air Force with a promise to see her soon.

That had been the last time she had seen him.

The night before he left for San Antonio, Texas. She still flushed at the memory of that night.

"So, Claire, what do you think?" Maine asked.

"They're impressive," she said, reining her thoughts back to the present.

He preened. Just a bit. But she saw it. "I'm inclined to celebrate," he said.

"That's a great idea," Claire agreed. "You should do that." Claire picked up his contract, turned to the signature page.

"You'll come with me," he said.

Claire smiled in an effort to turn around the anxiety that washed over her at his words. "Oh, no," she said, watching his expression change from friendly, excited artist to rejected man. If he pulled his paintings now, the whole fundraiser would crash and burn. There would be no mentorships. No scholarships. It would all be for naught. "I'll go next time. After the fundraiser. Right now I'm buried in paperwork and," she glanced at her watch. "I have to be up early for a meeting tomorrow." She lowered her voice. "And don't tell anyone, but alcohol gives me the worst possible headache you can imagine."

She sent up a silent prayer of thanks when he backed off, appeased, for the moment at least. He winked, clicked his tongue, and cocked a finger at her. "I'll hold you to that," he said.

Claire held her breath as he signed the contract. "Now, I have to get this to the fundraising attorney," she checked her watch again. "Before he leaves for the evening. We're on a strict deadline." She grabbed up her handbag, and, clutching the signed contract in her other hand, left him standing there in her own office.

Her heels clicked on the stairs as she raced down them and outside to her BMW sedan. She was in her car with the doors locked before she took a deep breath and pressed her hands against the steering wheel.

The paperwork could have easily waited until morning. Even Martie, her personal assistant, could have driven it over. Or they could have faxed a copy to lock in the contract.

She had just needed to get as far away from Maine D'Court as she could. Maybe tonight would be a good night to hibernate at home with some good undistracted rest and relaxation.

She sent Martie a quick text asking her to lock up. When Claire received an affirmative answer, she shoved the contract into her briefcase and headed home.

Claire parked in the garage, went inside, and greeted her silver Persian kitten. Charlie wasn't even a year old. He'd been her gift to herself after the divorce was finalized. She picked him up, and hugging him to her, took him into the kitchen to feed. She pulled the top on a can of kitten food and stirred it into a saucer.

Laughing at Charlie's barely audible meow, she ruffled his hair and watched him lap up the food.

She went upstairs, changed into her slim crop pants and a t-shirt. She went into her walk-in closet, keyed in the code to her wall safe, and took out a slim photo album.

She carried the photo album back downstairs, opened a bottle of Dakota Shy Cabernet Sauvignon, poured a glass, and curled up on her sofa.

Claire loved her house. She's chosen everything from the basic design to the doorknobs. She loved her over-the-top walk-in closet with shelves and drawers. She loved her kitchen with its huge windows overlooking a wooded back yard. She loved her fireplace with the plasma TV hanging on the wall over it.

She could open her iPad and close the shades on her windows, turn on her TV, and see if anyone was at the front door. All that technology blended seamlessly into a warm cozy environment. Her home was her haven – her safe place away from everyone where she didn't have to worry about saying the right thing or dressing a certain way.

Even when Danielle had friends over, she felt relaxed here. This was her space.

Charlie sat next to her on the floor and stared at her. She picked him up in one hand and put him on the sofa beside her. He slapped at the fringe on a throw she'd tossed across the back of the sofa, then curled into a ball next to her and fell asleep purring.

Claire sipped her wine, then taking a deep breath, opened the photo album. It had been a long time since she'd dared to open it up – probably fifteen years.

It was a photo album she'd started when she was sixteen years old. There were lots of pink hearts drawn with a felt tipped pin. On only the first page, Grayson smiled back at her.

Her heart skipped a little as she studied the picture of the two of them together. They looked so very happy with their arms wrapped around each other.

Claire had given up long ago trying to figure out what went wrong.

It had been so long – twenty years. Did it really matter anymore?

Seeing him today had brought butterflies back to her stomach. Butterflies she thought had flown years ago.

Danielle texted saying she was going out to dinner with her friends and would be home late.

Perfect. Claire had the whole evening to herself.

Claire flipped through the pages, allowing the memories to play through her mind. Some bringing a smile. Others bringing tears.

When the clock chimed seven o'clock, she closed the album and set it aside.

What were the odds that she'd run into Grayson Moore? Why today?

It doesn't matter. It's all in the past now.

And Claire Worthington kept her eyes on the future.

2

———————

The event was going to be a huge success. Claire could feel it. And she had an instinct for these things. The wine was flowing freely and the artist was charming. Women would be falling over themselves to transfer money. Already, he'd sold three paintings. His artistic style was conservative. The kind an older woman would want displayed in her home. Not too trendy and not the kind that would have shock value.

A few new people had come in that Claire needed to greet.

As she watched, a group of four split, leaving one standing alone as she approached.

Her heart tripped up a notch as she approached him. He stood staring at a painting with splashes of purple and red. Claire's favorite out of the ones the artist had contributed. He stood with his hands behind his back, his legs a few inches apart. Dark hair curled at his collar.

She stood next to him. Stared into his handsome face. How was it possible he had gotten more handsome than he was at eighteen? He was in his prime now, she admitted, her lips twitching up.

"I wonder why he named it *Fireworks*," he said.

"How did you find me?" she asked.

He shrugged, shifted his attention to her. Studied her as though she, too, were a thing to admire. "It wasn't hard."

"You like art?" she asked.

"I admire anything with beauty. Where did you go, Claire?"

"I didn't go anywhere," she said, feeling the lump in her throat. "Why did you disappear?"

"I was in the Air Force. You knew where I was."

"Not even once," she said. "You didn't write. You didn't call. Not even once."

The pain she felt saying those words out loud were reflected in his own features. "Of course I did."

"No," she said. "I would have known. I was right here. Waiting."

"Claire," he said. "I called you every chance I got. The calls were refused. Every time."

"No," she said.

"I called collect. I didn't have any other way to call you."

She wasn't sure how to respond. Why would he say that? Grayson had never been one to lie.

"Did you read my letters?" He asked. "I sent you information on how to contact me. But you didn't."

"What letters?"

"I wrote you letters and mailed them, mostly every week, at first anyway."

"Real letters?"

He scoffed. "Real letters. With stamps."

"You must have had the wrong address."

He recited her parents' home address. Claire felt a little light-headed. She needed to sit down, but instead, she took a deep breath and steadied herself. "I never got them," she breathed.

"Claire," he said. He almost reached for her, but instead, put his hands in his pockets.

"I have to… um…" She glanced around. "I have to see to my guests."

She had to think. And she couldn't think with him staring at her that way. Like he wanted to pull her to him and kiss all the years away.

She turned and walked across the room, keeping her head high. Her imagination was a thing to keep a tight leash on. At least where Grayson Moore was concerned. She put a smile on her face as she approached two middle-aged women standing in front of a very expensive painting.

Weekly etiquette classes for the last years of high school had taught her nothing if not how to hide her emotions. Miss Baker's voice still resonated in Claire's head. *Never let them see you sweat. Or cry. Or have uncontrollable laughter. In fact, always be in control.*

Emotional control was so ingrained in Claire's psyche, she wasn't sure she could be any other way.

By the time the evening was winding down, only one painting was left unsold. It was Claire's favorite – the purple and red one. The one the artist had named *Fireworks.*

The artist, Maine D'Court, was ecstatic. They had agreed that he would receive a small percentage of sales, but mostly he was trying to establish a name for himself. If tonight was any indication, he was well on his way to success.

The members of the Enrich American Minds Foundation were also elated. With the money earned tonight, they would be able to pick five high school students, mentor them through graduation, guide them into college, and provide tuition support.

Now the hard work started. Claire had to hire ten new mentors, two of whom would follow each student who was chosen.

Because of tonight, five students who never would have set

foot on a college campus would now have the opportunity to become college educated, productive members of society.

Claire walked around the gallery, reminding her committee members about their meeting Monday afternoon. She stopped in front of the *Fireworks* painting and wondered why it hadn't sold.

"Is this the only one left?" Grayson's voice was like a familiar balm settling over her soul.

"Yes," she said without turning around.

"I like it."

She turned then and looked into those blue eyes that had haunted her dreams for years. "It's curious that no one bought it."

"How much?"

She lifted an eyebrow.

"How much for the painting?"

"You don't want to buy it," she said turning back toward the painting, though her heart was racing and every cell was tuned towards Grayson's presence.

"How much?" he asked again.

"You can't afford it."

She counted to ten before turning back to him.

"I'm not eighteen anymore," he said.

She smiled. That was an understatement. Very well. She'd play along. She quoted him a figure.

He reached into his jacket pocket and pulled out a checkbook.

She was pleased that she managed to keep her jaw from dropping.

GRAYSON PRIDED himself on not flinching. There went two months' salary. This was retirement money, but still...

He'd heard Claire tell three different people that this was

her favorite painting by this artist. She hadn't said that about any of the others, so he felt confident that it was the truth.

As he wrote out the check, he wondered if that was why no one had bought it. Perhaps no one had the heart to buy it out from under her.

Grayson wasn't buying it out from under her. He was giving her a one hundred percent success rate tonight.

And he planned to give the painting to her when the time was right.

"Is this where you work?" he asked as he handed her the check. Surely he'd earned a bit of information by donating.

"Yes," she said. "My office is upstairs."

"Nice," he said, sweeping his gaze around the spacious, modern, gallery. A wide staircase led upstairs to an open area. Offices, he assumed and meeting space. It was impressive.

"Thank you," she said, a smile settling over her features. He liked the smile better than her consternation.

"Does Danielle still live at home?" he asked.

"Yes," she said.

She was making him ask. "Do you have other children?"

"No, just Danielle."

There was no one else within earshot. He had so many questions but he couldn't tell if he was making her uncomfortable or not. But she was still standing there, so he could only assume she was willing to talk with him. Claire had always been good at keeping her emotions in check. He knew she'd been schooled to do that. She was the rich girl. The one with every possible door of opportunity in front of her. He had been just a regular guy. Joining the Air Force to serve his country.

He'd often wondered if she was part of what drove him to keep bettering himself. He knew she was the reason he never married. He'd had girlfriends, sure, even lived with one of them, but none of them had ever been marriage material for

Grayson. Claire had ruined that for him. She had been the only one.

"Do you have children?" She asked, running her fingers along his check.

He shook his head. "No."

"Really? You wanted four."

I wanted four with you. "Things change," he said, the smile dropping from his lips. It was definitely better to talk about her. "And you wanted two."

"Things change," she said. Perhaps telling her about the letters, though she apparently hadn't gotten them, was helping to keep her here talking to him.

Maine D'Court approached, "Claire," he said, his voice silky.

"Maine," Claire said, shifting to include him in their conversation. "We just sold the last of your paintings," she nodded toward Grayson.

Grayson scowled. Had he really just given this man money? This slim man with a ponytail of all things. The military man in him cringed.

"Is that so?" Maine said. "Well, I hope you enjoy it."

"I'm sure I will," Grayson said, stretching to his full height of six feet. Maine was at least four inches shorter.

"I'll have your check for you early next week," Claire said, turning away slightly. Grayson gave her points for gracefully dismissing the man.

"Great," Maine said. "Let me know when you're ready to get out of here."

"Get out?" she echoed.

"Yeah. You owe me a drink, remember?"

Grayson saw the flash of panic shoot through her eyes. She didn't want to go with him.

She looked directly at him, a smile on her lips. "Not tonight, Maine."

"You promised."

She shook her head. "I already have plans," she said.

Grayson felt his muscles tense. It had been a few years since he'd been in a fight. Might feel good.

"You promised," he said, shoving a finger at her.

"Hey," Grayson said, stepping in front of Claire. "The lady said no. When a lady says no, she means no."

"We had plans," Maine said, trying to reach behind Grayson for Claire's hand. She stepped back before he could touch her.

"No," Grayson said, stepping front of Claire. "The lady is with me."

Maine glared at him, then at Claire, before, muttering, he walked away.

"He sure knows how to win friends," Grayson said.

"Thank you," she said, turning her gaze to Grayson.

"He has some nerve, doesn't he?"

"I'm afraid so," Claire said. "But I think he's harmless."

Maine, however, didn't leave. He sat on the stairs leading up to Claire's office. And watched them, his expression surly.

"I hope you're right," Grayson said. The gallery was nearly empty now. "If you don't mind, I'll hang around until you get to your car."

"I don't mind. I have to go up to my office for a few minutes before I leave."

"I'll go with you," Grayson said. He was relieved that she wasn't one of those women who didn't want protection from men. Grayson never understood that. What those women didn't understand was that they may be smarter than most men, but they would never have the testosterone to match. It was like a man who thought he could go up bare handed against a lion. The lion would always win.

Claire was smart though. The smartest woman Grayson had ever known.

Maine watched them, said nothing as they went upstairs to

her office. Grayson stood outside her door, bodyguard style while she gathered up what she needed to take with her.

Claire tossed papers into her briefcase. She planned to work from home this weekend, but she was having trouble thinking about what she need to take with her.

She was having trouble thinking about anything other than Grayson Moore standing outside her office door ready to protect her from an ardent admirer with an inflated self-esteem.

Had she been too friendly with Maine D'Court? She had promised to have a drink with him after the showing, but she hadn't meant right after on the same night. It had been intended as discouragement. Like *sure, we'll get together sometime and catch up* when both people knew that would never happen.

Claire tapped her fingers on the desk as she considered how she was going to get Maine D'Court out of her gallery without making a scene. It was because of him that tonight had been so successful. She didn't want to seem ungrateful. But it had been a business arrangement. He'd made a lot of money. Sold paintings he never would have sold. It was a win-win.

She was mostly cross with him because he was disrupting her thought process about Grayson. Grayson was the one she wanted to be thinking about. Not a narcissistic artist.

She gathered up her handbag and drew it over her shoulders. She was thankful Grayson was here tonight. She wasn't sure what she would have done about Maine D'Court. His persistence bordered on stalking.

Would she have to be afraid now? And afraid for Danielle?

As they walked back downstairs, side by side, Claire was struck by the familiarity of walking next to Grayson. He was a full head taller than she was. And, she readily admitted, she felt safe with him at her side.

Maine D'Court, however, was nowhere in sight. They did a quick search, but the building was empty.

Claire locked up with Grayson keeping watch. Their cars were the only two cars left in the parking lot. Maine D'Court, it seemed, had decided to go his own way.

Nonetheless, Grayson walked around her BMW and peeked through the glass into the backseat.

"Were you deployed?" she asked.

"You could say that. All in all, I spent about ten years overseas."

"Wow. That's a lot."

"I went to college here, though, at Stanford."

"Impressive."

"That's where you went, right?"

"I didn't go," she said.

"Oh," he said.

"I got married and started my business."

He gazed around, then pinned those blue eyes to hers. He was standing close now. So close, she could see the little lines around his eyes. Little lines that weren't there twenty years ago. "You never married?" she asked, her voice barely a whisper, dreading the answer.

"Nope. Hard to meet anyone when you're rarely home."

"Well, you were living overseas, right? And then college. Sounds like ample opportunity. A lot of soldiers get married while they're on tour of duty."

"I'm only interested in American girls. And college students were babies by the time I got there."

"Do you still see them that way?" she asked.

"Even more."

"That's probably a good thing since you're surrounded by college students all day long."

"Children," he said. "Are you going straight home?"

"I usually do."

"I'd ask if you wanted to get a dinner, but you already shot one guy down tonight."

She glanced at her watch. "It's a little late for dinner, isn't it?"

"I suppose so," he said, never taking his eyes off hers. "I hadn't noticed. I'm surely not going to ask you for drink."

She laughed. "Too bad," she said. "I would have gone." She slipped into her car and he closed the door.

She smiled as she drove away, enjoying the astounded expression on his face.

It took a full ten minutes for her heart rate to go back to a normal rhythm.

She'd never in a million years expected Grayson Moore to still be single after all these years. He must have women throwing themselves at him constantly. No one could look that good and be that gentlemanly and not have women after him.

He must have found out about her fundraiser through UCLA. Too late, she realized she should have asked. Ah well. Chances were good she wouldn't see him again unless she happened to run into him in Danielle's psychology building.

She had accounts to work on this weekend. And thank you letters to write. There was no time to dwell on the past. What was done was done.

GRAYSON WATCHED Claire drive out of the parking lot and resisted the urge to follow her. Maine D'Court was probably harmless. More bravado than any actual threat. Still, it wouldn't hurt for her to be vigilant until she was out of his crosshairs.

But mostly, he stood there, letting her words echo through his mind, sending little shock waves of unexpected pleasure. *I would have gone.*

And then he'd let her slip right through his fingers again. He *had* called her. Not right away and then once he was in Germany, using the phone became even more difficult. He mused that her consistent lack of response was most effective.

It had worked just like he taught in class. In fact, he sometimes used the example of trying to reach an old girlfriend as an example of extinction in his intro psychology classes. If she'd wanted to extinguish his attempts, she had certainly done it the right way. Absolutely no response. Not even once. However, just like he taught, he'd had spontaneous recovery. In textbook reaction, he'd shown up on her doorstep the day he got back from Germany. Her mother had told him she wasn't home. And suggested he not come back.

It had worked. He'd finally gotten the message. When a lady says no, she meant no. Still, there remained lingering doubt through the years. Doubt because he'd never actually spoken to Claire.

When his mother sent him the newspaper clipping of Claire's marriage to Noah Worthington, something in his heart had cracked. She could have at least told him.

Even though he moved on, he never found anyone he wanted to commit his life to. Claire had been it for him. His soul mate.

He'd come close a time or two, but something always interfered. When he didn't feel like blaming his lack of desire for marriage on Claire, he blamed it on the things he'd seen in Iraq and Afghanistan. Even without a diagnosis of PTSD, he knew it was normal to have difficulty with attachments.

Grayson hadn't even gone looking for Claire later on Facebook. If she was happily married, he certainly didn't want to be the one to create any doubt in her mind.

Now that he'd run across her and she was single again, all bets were off.

He drove the thirty minutes to his apartment near the university and went inside. He couldn't help imagining how

Claire might see his place. It was clean, but a little cluttered. He had the basics – TV, sofa, small dining room table. The apartment had come furnished, so he hadn't had any input into the décor. It hadn't seemed to matter. Until now.

He grabbed a bottle of water and settled on his sofa with his computer. He logged into the university website and typed in Danielle Worthington. It was so very easy to find Claire's address. *It's not stalking.* He just needed her address so he could send her the painting. After he wrote down her address, he exercised self-restraint. For all of three minutes.

Then he typed the address in google maps. Nice neighborhood. Lots of trees and space. And not so very far from the university. He estimated he could be there in fifteen minutes if she needed him.

He logged out of the university website and laughed at himself. Even if she needed him, she had no way to get in touch with him. His phone number wasn't on his check. He even had doubts that he would see her again. He'd found her easily enough just by googling her name. She was well-known in the fundraising community. It looked like she'd done well adding art to her method. He was impressed that she'd branched out from the usual charities to one that was personally near and dear to his heart – higher education. Higher education often got lost in the shuffle, but what she was doing was awe inspiring.

It was funny, he mused, how their minds had converged so many years after they'd disconnected. He was teaching college and she was raising money for students to attend. He was surprised she hadn't gone to college. She'd planned on it. But, marriage, it seemed, had taken precedence. There was no way to figure it out. He would have to talk with her to solve the mystery of her life.

She wouldn't have dinner with him, but she would have gone to have a drink with him. *If he'd asked.*

Claire had always been a mystery to him.

He had to tread carefully. He didn't want to repeat whatever mistake he'd made twenty years ago that had scared her away.

He'd start slowly.

He'd start with the painting.

3

Claire closed the lid on her computer and stretched. She'd been up since dawn and had been working nonstop for two hours. It had been a week since the fundraising event. She'd gotten tons of work done, but the week had been jam packed with meetings. So, as usual, she was spending Saturday morning working in her home office.

Feeling the need to stretch her legs, she got dressed in her tights, sports bra, and T-shirt. She laced up her running shoes and put in her earbuds. She went into her exercise room, turned on Taylor Swift, and hopped on the treadmill. She never warmed up. Warming up always seemed like a waste of time. She just took off running.

She was well into mile three when the doorbell rang. Danielle was still asleep and it was too early for any of her friends to be coming over. It was rare that anyone was up and about on a Saturday morning. Even the neighbors stayed to themselves.

She went to the door and peeked out through the glass. A courier stood there with a large package balanced against his legs. Oh no. Surely Maine D'Court didn't send her a painting.

She'd put his check in the mail, so he should have it now. She'd even added in a bonus for having a one hundred percent sell out. Maybe that had backfired and encouraged him. She'd hoped he would leave her alone now that the fundraiser was in the past.

She couldn't leave the courier standing on her front stoop all day. She opened the door and he slid what could only be a painting into her foyer and propped it against the wall. "These usually go to the gallery," she said, "Are you sure you have the right address?"

The boy showed her the address label. She didn't recognize the return address and there was no name listed. If this had been the gallery, she would have thought someone was sending her an unsolicited sample of their work. But for it to come to her home address was creepy.

She thanked the courier and locked the door. Then she ripped the thick paper from the painting and sat down on the stairs.

It was the fireworks painting. The very same painting she had personally sent to Grayson on Monday.

Unless…

She checked the back for the sticker she always added to indicate that it was purchased for the purpose of charity. And breathed a sigh of relief. The sticker was there. For a moment, she had feared that Maine D'Court had painted another just for her.

But this…

Grayson had spent a lot of money to buy this painting. And now he was just giving it away. She dug through the wrapping for a note, but there wasn't one. Nothing.

She stood with her hands on her hips. He could have at least sent his phone number along so she could call and thank him.

She should really send it back to him. It was too much to accept. But the thought made her giggle. They would quickly spend more on sending the thing back and forth than he'd paid for it to begin with.

When she had quoted the price, she didn't think he would actually buy it. If she'd thought he was going to buy it, she'd have taken off her commission, but then once he had his check book out, it would have been an insult to suddenly lower the price as though he couldn't afford to pay. In truth, she had no idea how much Grayson Moore could afford to pay.

"Mom?" Danielle called sleepily from the top of the stairs. "I thought I heard the doorbell. Is everything alright?"

"Everything's okay, honey," Claire said, reaching to pick up the wrapping paper. Charlie followed Claire down the stairs and rolled around in the paper, sending them both into a spell of giggles.

"What is that?" Danielle asked. "Is that from the fundraiser?"

"It is." Claire had no idea what to do with the painting.

"Did you buy it?" Danielle asked.

Claire shook her head.

"Who did?"

Claire looked at her daughter. She couldn't lie to her. "Grayson," she said.

Danielle's eyes widened. "No. Way."

"Way," Claire said, pulling on some twine to entertain the kitten.

"But…" She studied the painting. "If he bought it, why would he send it to you?"

"He probably overheard me telling someone that I liked it."

"So… he bought it for you," Danielle said, her lips turning into a smile.

Claire shrugged. "I guess."

"Do you like it? Really?" Danielle asked.

"Yeah. I do."

"We should put it in the kitchen," Danielle decided. "We need some color in there."

"Let's take it in there and see," Claire said.

The two of them carried the painting into the kitchen and stood it against the wall Claire had left bare. Danielle had been right. It did add a splash of color to the room.

"Nice," Danielle said. "Now tell me why my psych teacher would send you a painting."

"I have no idea," Claire went to turn on the tea kettle.

"Mom," Danielle said in a voice much too old for her eighteen years.

Claire pulled two mugs from the cabinet. "Alright," she said. How much did she tell her daughter? The truth, but not everything. Just like with Noah.

"We dated in high school."

Danielle gasped. "You did not!"

Claire smiled as she sipped water.

"Wait," Danielle grew serious. "I know that look. Is Grayson my father?"

Claire coughed as the water went down the wrong way. "Heavens, no. Noah is your father, honey."

"That's good," Danielle said. "But if you married Grayson, I'd have two awesome fathers."

"I can't believe you just said that," Claire said, but the idea latched onto her own fantasies.

"Why not? He's so much fun."

"I haven't even seen him in twenty years."

"Looks like he noticed you."

Claire flushed. Only out of the mouths of children. Especially almost adult children who had been in intensive therapy for almost a year and had learned to say what they felt.

"You should call him," Danielle said.

"I don't have his number."

Danielle tugged on the twine and laughed as the cat leaped into the air to grab it. She looked back at Claire, a smile on her lips. "I do."

Claire hadn't thought of that. She could call Grayson at his office. Fortunately for her, it was Saturday, so he wouldn't be there.

"I have his cell number," Danielle said.

Claire nearly dropped the tea kettle. "What? How?"

Danielle shrugged. "It's on the syllabus."

"He put his cell number on his syllabus?" She asked as she poured water into their mugs for tea.

"Sure. It's no big deal. It's not like anyone will call him. They'll just send texts."

"I didn't know they did that," Claire murmured. Texting a professor seemed like such an invasion of privacy. Especially texting a man who didn't even have a cell phone the last time she knew him.

She took a deep breath. "I could text him."

"Are you kidding? Mom. You can't text a thank you for a gift like that. I know how much your paintings go for. Seriously?"

"You're right."

"You're scared."

"I am not," Claire said. She so was.

"I'll get you the number," Danielle said, with a mischievous smile. "But you don't have to call him if you don't want to. I'm sure you'll do what's right."

It was so strange to hear her own words coming back to her from the one she'd said them to so many times before.

Danielle's phone rang. Claire recognized the ring tone Danielle had picked for her father. Noah called his daughter several times a week. Danielle's suicide attempt had been a wake-up call for all of them.

She took her tea and sat at the little table in the kitchen nook and watched the birds flutter around the bird feeder. The bird feeder she'd forgotten to fill.

The housekeeper was coming today. She'd put it on her list. Claire needed a shower before she called Grayson.

And, yes, she would call him. It was the right thing to do.

CLAIRE CALLED at eleven o'clock to thank him for the painting. She said she would text a picture over once she had it on the wall. It might be awhile.

She said she and Danielle were about to have lunch and go to the mall. One of Danielle's friends was coming along.

Grayson enjoyed the easy conversation between them. Unfortunately, it was all too brief.

He hadn't known if she would call. He hadn't given her his phone number on purpose. He didn't want it to be too easy… or too obvious. He also knew that his cell phone was on his syllabus. The only way she would get it would be if she talked to Danielle about him. It meant she told Danielle who'd sent the painting. It was important that Danielle be included in this new relationship with Claire.

Claire and Danielle were a package deal now. He knew that up front. And he wanted to make sure Claire knew he knew it.

He closed the textbook he'd been reading. He was distracted now and there was no way he was going to be able to concentrate. He saved Claire's phone number in his phone, put on some shorts and his running shoes and headed out for a jog.

Jogging cleared his head when nothing else would. He jogged down the sidewalk to the park and let his mind wander as he joined the Saturday morning families out for some sunshine. It was hot, but nothing like the south where he'd been stationed the last couple of years. San Antonio was hot. After lunch, jogging was prohibitive, to say the least. But here the weather was nice comparatively.

Claire said she never got his letters. He had the address right. What could have happened?

Her parents had seemed to like him well enough. But with him out of the way, it was hard to say what had happened. He'd googled the Worthington family after his mother had sent him the article about Claire's wedding. The Worthington family of Ft. Worth was wealthy to say the least. He couldn't blame Claire's father if he'd managed to arrange a marriage for her with someone of wealth.

Grayson certainly couldn't have offered her the lifestyle she was used to. He came from an upper middle-class family. He was doing okay now with his retirement from the military and his salary from the university. But still, he couldn't put himself in the wealthy category.

It was fortuitous that Claire was divorced now that he was back in town. It was even more fortuitous that Claire's daughter was in his class. Grayson had only been teaching for one year, starting last fall. The only way it could have been weirder was if she'd shown up in his very first class.

Grayson had learned a long time ago not to push things. If something was going to happen, it would happen. If he tried to push it and make it happen, it would only turn out badly.

He'd shown up at Claire's fundraiser, he'd bought the painting, and he'd sent it to her.

It was time to back off.

He wasn't putting the ball in her court. That wouldn't be fair. She'd done nothing to deserve that kind of treatment. Especially when she didn't know the rules.

But he would lay off for a while. Let things simmer. She was newly divorced. She didn't need him pushing at her.

Besides, August 3 was his last day in Los Angeles. Grayson would have finished his one year visiting professorship and had accepted a one-year full-time teaching position at Robert Morris University in Pittsburgh.

4

*C*laire went upstairs knowing she would find her mother in the sitting room on the third floor of her home. Since her father had died three years ago, her mother had happily retreated from the hectic society life and spent her days mostly reading and sometimes sending emails and Facebooking with old friends.

The small sitting room, twice as large as most apartments, was not only spacious, but serene. Her mother had a flair for decorating that led to a calm atmosphere. Claire wondered how long it would be before her mother sold the large, cumbersome house where she had lived so many years with her husband and move into a smaller, more manageable place. Of course, with a live-in housekeeper, a cook, and a variety of other hired help, Claire mused that it probably didn't matter much. Her mother could live on the third floor of the house and the rest of the house would sustain itself. She even had a personal assistant who paid the bills and handled the business side of running a household including shopping for staples.

Claire had a personal assistant, too, but the girl, Martie,

mostly handled business administrative work. And errands. Claire hated errands. The driving. The in and out of the car kind of errands. She had a weekly dry cleaning delivery service and basic food delivery, so Martie really had a limited number of errands.

"Claire," her mother smiled and stood up to hug her. "Did Danielle come?"

Danielle and Betty had been fast friends since the day Danielle came into the world.

Claire supposed it was a natural since Claire spent so much time working and Betty kept her during the weekdays when Danielle wasn't in school.

"She's got her afternoon yoga class and then she's going out with some friends."

"Aw," Betty sank back into her chair. "Tell her to come by when she has time."

"You know you'll see her this weekend."

"It's never soon enough," Betty said. "What brings you out here on a Tuesday?"

Her mother wanted to cut to the chase then. "I wanted to talk to you about something."

"All right. Would you like something to drink?"

Claire shook her head. "I have water."

"What's on your mind?"

"Do you remember Grayson?"

Her mother's face went blank. How could she not remember Grayson? Claire had been going to marry him.

"Of course," Betty said.

"He said he called."

Betty didn't even pretend not to know what Claire was talking about. Betty looked away, seeming to gaze at a bouquet on her desk.

"Did he?" Claire asked, her voice soft.

"He did. He called collect a few times. I didn't take the calls. Then he stopped."

"Mother. Why did you refuse his calls?"

"He was military," her mother said, turning back to face Claire. "You would have been part of another lifestyle. I didn't want that for you."

"Another lifestyle?"

"The military. I didn't think you would fit in."

Claire scoffed. "Shouldn't I have been the one to decide that?"

Betty sighed. "Probably. But I knew you weren't in a place to decide. You were too in love."

"Mom." Claire leaned forward in her chair. "What's wrong with love?"

Betty leaned away. "Do you remember I had a sister?"

"Of course. Aunt Mary. She died when I was… six? I was in first grade."

"Yes. She was older than I was. 8 years older. She was in love with a boy in the Army. He was drafted and they were married immediately." Betty took a deep breath. Kept going. "She got pregnant. Her husband was killed over there. In Vietnam. It broke Mary's heart. She took her own life and that of the child."

"Oh no," Claire pressed her fingertips against her forehead. Remembered all the forms she'd lied on. In both Ft. Worth and here. *Has anyone in your family ever committed suicide?*

She'd answered *no* on each and every one. How many staff members had mentioned that suicide runs in families? "What didn't you tell me?" she asked and looked up at her mother, knowing the hurt was naked in her eyes. "Danielle…"

"I thought that if no one knew, it would be better."

"But when Danielle…"

"I know. I didn't say anything. I know they say it runs in families. But my therapist told me that it wasn't genetic. It was learned through environment. He said it was better if I didn't say anything."

"Danielle doesn't stand a chance."

"No! Don't think like that."

Claire straightened in her chair. Lifted her chin. "What does this have to do with Grayson?"

"Oh." Her mother fiddled with the handle on her desk drawer. "Every time I thought about the Army, I got sick to my stomach. Still do."

"So you punished me?"

"When Grayson said he was going into the Air Force, I couldn't stomach the thought of you being part of that world. I couldn't stand the thought of you living your life in misery."

"But you encouraged me to marry Noah." Claire said. Would her mother get the implication that she'd ended up in misery after all.

Her mother paled. "Yes," she uttered.

Claire shook her head and turned away. She fought the host of conflicted emotions that threated to overwhelm her.

"Was it really that bad?" Betty asked.

"No," Claire admitted. "It wasn't that bad being with Noah. We hardly ever saw each other. But, Mother, you kept me away from Grayson."

Her mother slowly reached for the bottom desk drawer handle and pulled it open. "I was going to wait and let you find these after I was gone." She reached into the back of the drawer. "But I have a feeling you need these now." She pulled out a two-inch stack of letters tied together with a ribbon and set them on the edge of the desk in front of Claire.

Claire stared at the stack of letters – at her name and parents' address scrawled across the front. And Grayson's name at the top. The letters were unopened. A weight sat in the pit of her stomach. A weight that carried regret and sadness. As the emotions settled in her gut, they released a new emotion.

Hope.

"Hı."

Grayson was in the middle of a department meeting when Claire called. They were discussing the summer advising schedule. None of the full-time faculty really wanted to be there. As the visiting faculty member, Grayson was sure he'd draw the short straw anyway, so when Claire's name came up on his phone, he stepped out.

"Is this convenient?"

"Sure," he lied. It had been just over two weeks since he'd sent her the painting.

"I won't keep you long. I was just wondering if you'd like to meet." She paused. "For that drink."

"Sure," he said. "When?"

"How about tonight?"

He had so much to do this weekend, it was going to be impossible for him to even come close to catching up. "Okay," he said. "Want me to pick you up?"

"No," she said. "I'll meet you. How about D'Vine's at seven o'clock?"

"I'll be there," he said.

He went back into the conference room and he was the only one smiling through the rest of the meeting. He ended up taking the most summer office hours, but not even that could spoil his good mood.

After the meeting, he googled the address for D'Vine's before swinging by his apartment for a quick shower and change of clothes.

He got to the D'Vine lounge at six and found a bistro table toward the back so he could watch the door for Claire. He ordered some bread and a glass of wine while he waited.

He'd almost given up on hearing from Claire. He'd been

toying with the idea of calling her. To take her up on that comment she'd made about having a drink with him. He certainly wasn't going to let her go that easily. In fact, his resolve to not push at her had been quickly fading.

There had been something in her voice when she'd called that he couldn't put his finger on. She sounded... serious. If he'd been contacting her, he would have worried that she wanted him to leave her alone. She'd sounded that serious. Right now, he was thankful he hadn't pushed at her.

Other than that, he was at a loss. Perhaps she was a much more serious person than before. When they dated in high school, she'd always had a smile in her voice. Except for the day before he left. In retrospect, sleeping together the night before he shipped out probably hadn't been the best idea.

He'd often wondered if that was why she didn't take his calls or answer his letters.

He'd done the math. Danielle was definitely not his child.

She walked in the door fifteen minutes early. It was going to take awhile to get used to her being brunette. She carried herself with different kind of confidence she'd had in high school. In school she'd been a bubbly majorette. Now she was a confident businesswoman.

He stood up so she would see him. She smiled and walked toward him. His attraction for her had never dimmed. He wondered how much his life was about to change with just this one meeting.

He held the bar stool while she climbed up, then sat next to her. "What would you like to drink?" he asked.

"A glass of chardonnay," she said.

He ordered her drink and another one for himself. They sat in silence for a couple of minutes before she lifted her gaze to his.

"I finished reading your letters," she said.

A jolt of surprise and trepidation shot through him. Surely

she wouldn't hold something he'd written twenty years ago against him.

"But… you said you never got them."

"I didn't. But my mother did."

It had been her mother all along. He'd suspected her father, but it hadn't really occurred to him that her mother might be the one against him.

"She decided I wouldn't make a good military wife," she scoffed.

"Wow," he said.

She lifted her eyes, wide with unshed tears. "I'm sorry," she said.

"You have nothing to be sorry about," he said.

A single tear dripped down her cheek. He reached out and gently swept it away with a finger. "Don't be sad," he said.

"Your letters," she said. "What you wrote was so very heart wrenching. You must have been devastated when you didn't hear from me."

"You could say that," he said. "But it was a long time ago. Time heals."

She took a deep breath. "Yeah."

"You must have been deeply hurt when you didn't hear from me."

She nodded. "I was. My parents convinced me that I would never hear from you again and that I should move on."

"They made sure you didn't hear from me," he said.

"It was a terrible thing they did."

The server brought their wine. Claire sipped, then set her glass down.

"I don't hold it against them," he said. "They were only looking out for you."

"Ha. Sometimes it's better if parents don't interfere." She rested her hands on the table, running her fingertip along a crack in the wood.

He reached out and put his hand over hers. "You have Danielle," he said. "And the future is bright."

CLAIRE WONDERED that either of them was willing to talk to the other. He believed that she hadn't responded to his letters while she believed he hadn't bothered to write or call. All this happened when they were most vulnerable. They had been young and had just slept together for the first time.

Both of them stabbed in the heart. But twenty years had passed. And Grayson was right. Time did heal. If it didn't heal, it did at least dull.

Had they been given a second chance? Claire wondered.

"Danielle said you recently retired from the Air Force. Have you been in this whole time?"

"I did twenty years. I won't say I loved every minute of it, but I got a college degree out of it and a nice retirement."

"You said you spent a lot of time overseas."

"A lot."

"What was your job?"

"I was a PJ," he said, then clarified. "Pararescue. Search and rescue."

"Impressive," she said.

"It was different."

"I can't even imagine."

"I wouldn't want you to. In some ways, your mother was right. The military is no place for having a family."

"Maybe," she said, still lost in the haze of his letters.

"Does the painting fit with your décor or is it a sore thumb?"

"It fits," she said, tapping her wine glass with a well-manicured fingernail. "Unfortunately, it's still sitting on the floor."

"It is kind of big," he agreed. "Would you like me to hang it for you?"

"Sure," she said. "But I don't want to impose."

"It's not an imposition, I promise," he assured her. "Have you eaten?"

"I had a snack," she said.

"Me too. Want to get dinner?"

She searched his eyes. Seemed to contemplate her answer. "Okay. I can do that," she said.

He laughed. "Nothing like a little enthusiasm."

She chuckled with him. "I'm sorry. I'm not the best of company right now. I just read two year's worth of letters from an old boyfriend."

"Prolific little guy wasn't he?"

"Maybe he should have been a writer," Claire said.

"I do write my share of research papers."

"A little different, I hope."

"A whole lot different."

She took a second sip of wine. "I'm sure your papers are well written."

"Yeah." He, too, sipped his wine, set down the glass, and kept his eyes down. His forehead was creased right in the middle. Worry lines that were in the process of etching a permanent home.

Even now, after twenty years, she knew him well enough to know something was troubling him. "What's bothering you?" she asked.

He shook his head. Glanced at her, then scoffed, and held her gaze. "I need to tell you something."

"That sounds ominous," she said and braced herself for whatever it was that had him in knots. Perhaps he had a terminal illness or perhaps he was gay. Whatever it was, she had a feeling it didn't bode well.

"It's about my job," he said.

She relaxed a bit.

"I have a master's degree in social work which allows me to teach psychology, but it's hard for me to find a full-time teaching position."

"I'm listening," she said.

"This job at UCLA is what they call a visiting professorship which is a nice way to say I get to work full-time but only for a year. I've managed to land a full-time teaching position."

"Congratulations!" she said.

"Thank you," he said.

"But…"

He scrubbed a hand across his chin. "It's in Pittsburgh, Pennsylvania."

Claire kept her emotions in check. On the outside. On the inside, her little bubble of hope burst, splattering her dreams and sending her thoughts down a familiar path from twenty years earlier.

They'd been sitting outside, at the park. It was early Spring, so the weather had been cool. Claire had been content, sitting there on a blanket, reading, with Grayson stretched out beside her. She'd thought he was sleeping.

"I'm going to be leaving soon," he had said.

"What?" She'd put her book aside and looked down at him. His eyes were closed.

"For Basic Training."

What felt like a knife had stabbed through her heart. She still remembered that feeling. She knew he'd joined the Air Force, but was hoping that he wouldn't have to actually go anywhere. "Where?" She asked.

"San Antonio."

She remembered staring straight ahead. Telling herself not to react. She'd been schooled in keeping her emotions in check.

But he was going away and there was nothing she could do to stop it.

The same feelings washed over her now. Grayson was going away and there was nothing she could do to stop it.

"When do you leave?" She asked, the déjà vu clogging her throat.

"August 3."

She swallowed, allowing the sadness to wash over her. It would pass.

But she needed to get away. She slipped off the bar stool, grabbed her handbag, and straightened her jacket. "I 'um. I need to go," she said, simply.

She rushed outside, dodging people, she barely saw. The only thought that consumed her was the need to get away.

She got into her car and sat, staring blankly ahead.

The tears threatened to spill from her eyes. Something wasn't right. She hadn't felt this intensity of emotion even through her divorce.

There had been only two times in her life that she'd felt this way. When Danielle attempted suicide and the day Grayson left over twenty years ago.

GRAYSON PAID the check and walked out onto the street.

When he'd entered the Air Force all those years ago, he'd been excited. He'd expected to finish up boot camp, then tech school, then get Claire, marry her, and take her wherever he went next. Six months at the most away from her.

Such was the innocence of youth.

He'd done everything he knew to do at the time to keep her. But he'd been so wrapped up in his career. Once he'd become pararescue, he hadn't had the time to think about much of anything else. The job had consumed his life.

He couldn't shake the feeling, however, that he'd let Claire slip through his fingers.

In the back of his mind, he'd always thought he would

someday come back to her and whisk her away. He supposed to be honest with himself, he'd imagined her waiting for him.

All that had changed when he'd gotten the newsletter article about her marriage. He'd thrown himself into work even more then.

He'd gotten a Silver Star and a host of other awards. Awards that didn't mean anything at the end of the day. He'd been awarded for doing his job.

And now what did he have to show for it?

What he didn't have was Claire.

And now history was repeating itself. His job was taking him away from her.

And just like last time, he wanted to spend as much time with her as he could before he left.

It was selfish, yes. But he was drawn to her.

Now that they were adults, there would be no parents keeping them apart. They had cell phones. He could text her and know that she got the message. Or he could pick up the phone and call her.

It wouldn't be like last time.

He got into his car and buckled up. He couldn't let her slip through his fingers again.

Seeing her was a sign. A sign that they still had a chance.

He typed the address that he had memorized into his GPS and headed toward her house.

As he went through the gates into her community, he was reminded that he may have a Silver Star awarded by the President of the United States, a master's degree, and a respected job in the community, but he would never live in her world.

He pulled into her circle drive and sat. This is where he could walk away. Go on about his life and let her go on with hers. It was the easy, uncomplicated thing to do.

Or... he could get out, walk up to her door, and complicate things for both of them.

Grayson groaned. He'd never chosen the easy way to do anything.

The least he could do was to hang the damn painting he'd bought for her.

5

———

Claire went straight to her bathroom and washed her face. She hated the way she'd left Grayson. It was so uncharacteristic of her.

But she'd needed to get away.

It was as though she was reliving the whole thing all over again. His whole leaving her behind again.

It had been so long ago, yet it seemed as though it was happening again.

It didn't matter that she now knew he had written her letters and tried to get in touch with her. Her heart remembered only the pain.

She changed into casual pants and T-shirt. She never should have asked him to meet her for drinks.

What was in the past was in the past.

She knew better than to walk backwards. Walking backwards always led to bumping into something. Someone always got hurt.

Focus on today.

Focus on what she could control. Not what she couldn't. He was moving away.

Again.

He had shown up in her life again just long enough to give her some closure. At least now she knew. She knew he hadn't just abandoned her.

If anything, she had abandoned him.

Maybe she should have tried harder.

She thought about Danielle.

Would she be willing to lie to her own child as her parents had lied to her?

If she believed it was for Danielle's good, she might.

Danielle had had several boyfriends over the last couple of years, but no one serious enough to consider marrying.

Perhaps her mother had been right to keep her from marriage at such a young age. It was something she could have believed if her mother hadn't turned right around and practically shoved her at Noah.

Claire had liked Noah. He was handsome and charming.

And if it hadn't been for Grayson, she probably would have fallen in love with him.

Instead, she'd kept her emotional distance and poured herself into starting her business.

It was how she'd coped with Grayson's leaving her behind and, as she believed, not even trying to contact her after she'd slept with him.

As she went downstairs, her doorbell rang.

She peeked through the one-way glass on the door and her pulse rate quickened.

Grayson stood there, his hands in his pockets, and concern on his face.

Taking a deep breath and releasing it in a sigh, she opened the door. And they stood looking at each other.

"I promised to hang that painting for you," he said.

"Yes, you did," She stepped back and a smile tugged at her lips.

He came inside and she closed the door. "Claire. I..."

He lifted a hand, but she turned away. "It's back here," she said.

Her blood pounded in her ears. She stopped in front of the painting and swiped at her hair. If she'd known Grayson Moore was going to be here, in her house, she wouldn't have changed into her crop pants and or washed the make-up from her face.

After seeing the painting propped there against the wall, he turned and swept his gaze around her kitchen.

Though she was proud of her house and loved the choices she'd made in designing it, it mattered very much to her what Grayson thought.

"Nice," he said.

"Thank you," she said.

"Whoever did the design did an awesome job."

"That would be me," she said.

He turned his focus back to her. "You?"

"Yeah," She felt the heat rise in her cheeks.

"You're full of surprises," he said, his voice husky.

She bit her lip. "I have a hammer," she said, opening a kitchen drawer with an impressive array of tools – hammer, screwdriver, level, nails, measuring tape, and even a laser level.

"Let me see what you have in there," he said, quickly becoming intimate with the contents of what she thought of as her tool drawer.

He took the hammer and found a couple of sturdy nails. "Do you have a pencil?"

"Of course," She grabbed a pencil from her kitchen desk and handed it to him.

"You want it about here?" He asked, after measuring the height of the painting.

"That looks good. Centered."

"Hold these nails," he said. She held out her palm as he

placed the nails in her hand. His hand hovered there, his knuckles against her palm, sending little shock waves through her. It was the first physical contact they'd had in over twenty years.

His gaze glued to hers, he released the nails and pulled his hand away.

Her nerves tingled. And she couldn't think. He measured and marked, then took the hammer and after a few quick strikes, had two nails in the wall. He picked up the heavy painting and easily slipped the wires over the nails.

He stepped back, straightened the painting. "How's that?" He asked.

She blinked and forced herself to focus on the painting. "It's perfect," she said. Even if he'd hung it upside down, it would have been perfect in her eyes at that moment.

"Do you need me to do anything else?" He asked.

Kiss me.

The thought came out of nowhere and jarred her out of her trance. "No," she said. "Thank you for doing that."

"It was the least I could do after buying the thing."

Claire chuckled. "As Danielle says, it adds a splash of color to the room."

"Has he bothered you anymore?" he asked.

"Maine D'Court? No."

"Good. I was afraid I was going to have to embarrass him."

She laughed. "Would you like some hot tea?"

"Sure," he said.

GRAYSON SETTLED on Claire's sofa with a cup of hot tea in his hands. He'd never had hot tea in his life. Claire's place was spotless. There was no way he could let her go to his place now. He had papers and books strewn everywhere.

She looked relaxed. She was wearing casual gray pants that

looked like a cross between sweat pants and tights with a light pink T-shirt. She'd scrubbed her face free of make-up before he got there leaving her smelling like soap.

He didn't want to leave. He just wanted to be near her. He'd ask to dinner, but she looked like she'd already settled in for the evening. With two sisters, he knew better than to even bring it up.

"Do you want to order a pizza and watch a movie?"

She pulled her feet under her and smiled. "Sure." Her kitten, Charlie, had exhausted himself running and playing and was curled up in her lap.

How many nights in high school had they had gotten pizza and watched a movie? It was the most normal thing he could think of.

She'd told him Danielle was out with friends and wouldn't be home until much later.

She picked up her iPad and clicked on the screen. "Do you still like Hawaiian pizza?" she asked, looking up at him.

"Yeah. Good memory," he said.

Smiling, she made a few more clicks. "The pizza should be here in about fifteen minutes." She clicked some more and the TV came on displaying the image on her iPad. "What would you like to watch?" she asked.

Grayson was impressed. "You pick," he said.

"All right." She pulled up a series called *The 100.* "I've been thinking about starting this series. Danielle has been watching it and loves it. I've been needing to catch up so I can watch it with her or at least talk with her about it."

"Sounds good," he said. "Let's do it."

She was curled up on her side of the sofa and he on the other side. She had her feet tucked under her and a pillow hugged under her chin.

It was comfortable. Almost familiar. Except she should have been sitting next to him with his arms around her.

But she was skittish. She'd run away from him twice already. Once in the museum and once at the lounge. Maybe three times if he counted the York and Orleans where they'd met. He was fairly certain she'd seen him and ducked into the restroom while Danielle walked over to introduce her.

He didn't blame her. Couldn't blame her. They'd been something like star-crossed lovers the last time around. He was glad they'd gotten to straighten out the misunderstanding. They'd been kids with her parents doing what she thought best for her daughter. Life had moved forward.

This was either a second chance to begin again or a chance for closure. He wasn't sure which one yet. He was leaning toward the second chance to start over.

When the doorbell rang, they both got up to go to the door to get the pizza.

"Hi Gregory," Claire said.

"Hi Mrs. Worthington." The delivery boy glanced at Grayson, then tried to look behind Claire. "Is Danielle home?"

"No, sorry. She's out tonight."

"Oh, well," he glanced at Grayson again. "Tell her I said hi."

"I will."

Grayson pulled some tip money out of his pocket and handed it to Gregory. "Thank you, sir," he said.

After Gregory left, Grayson carried the pizza into the living room while Claire went to the kitchen to get plates.

"You know you're getting older when the pizza delivery guy calls you sir," he said when she came back with plates and two bottles of water.

"Wait until you have a child," she said. "Then you really get used to it."

Grayson didn't respond. He focused on sorting through the pizzas. "You're still vegetarian," he said, noting her cheese pizza.

"And sometimes vegan," she said.

"Vegan is hard," he commented.

"Yeah. It's not so bad here, but in Ft. Worth it's almost impossible to be vegetarian, much less vegan."

"Beef country."

"You have no idea."

"How long have you had this place?" he asked.

"A couple of years. I started building it while Noah and I were still married. He didn't even know it."

Grayson filled his plate, sat back and took a bite. "This is good," he said. "You must have felt like you were living a double life."

"I did. Most people wondered why I would do that. Why I would have a life without Noah even knowing about it."

"That is something to wonder about," he said.

"It wasn't that Noah was too busy. We're all busy. I think it's just because he wasn't here. He was gone more than he was home."

"Still," Grayson said. "It seems like it would have been worth a conversation."

"We had a strange relationship, Noah and me. It was more of an arranged marriage than a marriage made in love."

"I kind of wondered about that. But you had a choice. Right?"

"Of course. But everyone wanted me to do it. And..." she took a bite and kept her eyes down.

He finished her sentence for her. "And I wasn't here."

"Pretty much," she said.

"You kind of have a trend going."

"Ha. Not a good thing."

"I'm sorry," he said.

"Not your fault."

"But it was about me," he said. "So, I'm sorry."

"I forgive you," she said, meeting his gaze.

"And I forgive you," he said, a mischievous grin on his face.

She smiled. "So, what, we just play it all over again? Hang out until you leave?"

"I don't know," he admitted. "I guess we just see what happens."

She considered. Nodded. "Might be better if we not repeat that last night."

She remembered. Of course she remembered. A woman always remembered her first time. As did a man.

"Deal," he said. "Do you like the show?" He asked, deliberately changing the subject.

"I do. Boys aren't very smart."

"I've always said girls are smarter than boys."

"As a rule, I agree."

"I believe it," he said.

They finished their pizza and Claire carried pizza boxes while Grayson carried plates to the kitchen and began putting them in the dishwasher.

Claire's phone rang. She frowned and answered. Her face went pale. "Where did you say?" She asked.

"Is she okay?" Claire closed her eyes and swayed a little, steadying herself with a hand on the counter. "I'll be right there."

"What is it?" Grayson asked.

She shook her head. "Danielle was in an accident."

CLAIRE WAS TREMBLING. She needed to find her handbag, but she couldn't remember where she left it. She paced to the living room, then back to the kitchen before she remembered that she kept her purse upstairs in the closet. She raced upstairs, grabbed her purse, and raced back down.

Grayson stood there, keys in his hand. "Come on," he said, taking her hand. "I'll drive."

Claire started to protest. The words formed on her lips, but she couldn't get them out loud. She let him lead her to his car and help her inside.

"Where?" he asked.

She told him the address and he took off driving. "Tell me what happened," he said as he drove.

She sat tensed on the edge of the seat. "I don't know. There was a car accident." She bit her thumbnail. "They said she was okay."

"We'll be there in a minute," he said.

Claire knew it would be more than a minute. It had been less than a year ago – last fall, that she'd ridden in the ambulance with Danielle after she drank too much vodka and took too many pills. Claire kept her Xanax locked in a safe now and rarely took it. She'd rarely taken it anyway. She'd only filled it because the doctor had insisted it would help with sleep. But Claire didn't like being knocked out. She liked being in control. If Danielle needed her or even her mother, she wanted to be alert in an instant.

Had Danielle tried to hurt herself again? She seemed to be doing so well. Her doctors seemed pleased with her progress. They'd told her that some adolescents go through that sort of thing, then never have any other problems. It was all about being aware. Being aware of signs and triggers. And getting help right away.

Claire hadn't seen any signs. And there hadn't been any triggers. Except for Danielle starting college, but she was excited. Claire was pretty certain about that.

"Hey," Grayson said. "I'm right here. You're not alone."

She brought her attention back to the moment. Focused her gaze on Grayson. "Thank you," she whispered.

He reached over and took her hand in his. "They said she was okay." He glanced at her reassuringly, then put his eyes back on the traffic.

They rode in silence the rest of the way to the hospital.

"I'll let you out," he said, dropping her off at the door to the ER. "I'll find you," he said as she jumped out and sprinted toward the doors.

Claire ran to the desk and asked for her daughter. The receptionist tapped on the computer, asked for Claire's name and then promptly ushered into one of the exam rooms. When she stepped through the door, Danielle was sitting on the edge of an exam table. "Mom!" She said. Danielle was being examined by a young male doctor.

Claire ran to her and squeezed her hand. "What happened, Baby?"

"I was riding with some girls across campus and we were hit by another car."

Claire felt a tear spill down her cheek. Her baby wasn't safe anywhere. Not even at school.

"She has a clavicle contusion," the doctor said.

"It means she has a bruised collarbone," Grayson said. All eyes turned on him. "Right?"

"Yes," the doctor said. "I'm going to wrap this bandage around you. You need to try and not move your arm more than necessary for about two weeks."

"What does that mean?" Danielle asked. "Not more than necessary?"

"It means take it easy," the doctor said, glancing at Grayson and fastening the ends of the bandage.

"I'll wait outside," Grayson said.

"No," Claire said, reaching for his hand. She needed his strength.

"Mom," Danielle said, "I'm okay. But I do need to get dressed now."

"We'll be right outside the door."

She stepped outside with Grayson and he pulled her close. She fit just like she remembered. Just under his chin. He held on tight.

"What does it mean? A bruised collarbone?" she asked against his chest.

"It means she didn't break her collarbone which is certainly a good thing. It means she's going to be in pain and have some swelling. She can use ice for the swelling, but she'll need to keep it in a sling to keep from moving it around too much. She should be back to normal with a week or two."

"It doesn't sound too bad."

"You might want to keep her home in the bed or on the sofa for a few days especially while she takes pain medication."

"Okay," she said, taking a deep breath.

"Is there something you haven't told me?"

"I wouldn't know where to start," she said.

He pushed back and lifted her chin until her eyes met his. "Start with Danielle," he suggested.

"Last Fall she attempted suicide."

"Oh Claire," he said, pulling her against him again and stroking the back of her head.

It felt good to have someone to lean on. "She needs to call her father," she said, trying to push back.

He held tight. "She can call on the way home. Or in the morning. Claire. She's okay."

He felt her nodding against his chest. "On the way home. Noah will want to know." *Unless he's flying and doesn't have phone service.*

The doctor left and Claire went back to help Danielle get dressed.

"Grayson came with you," Danielle observed.

"He did."

"How did that happen?" Danielle asked.

"He came over to help me hang the painting."

Danielle grinned, then groaned when she moved her arm wrong. "The doctor wrote a script for pain pills, but I'm not going to take them."

"Why not?"

"I don't wanna be a pill head."

Claire hid a smile. Perhaps all that therapy had done some good.

"Is Grayson coming back with us?" she asked.

"He drove me here, so yes."

"Good."

"You're enjoying this," Claire observed.

Danielle shrugged. Groaned. "It's cute."

Cute. Claire rolled her eyes, but as they got Danielle up and into the wheelchair, her eyes teared up. The memory of her daughter on life support was too fresh.

As soon as they hit the door, Grayson grabbed the handles on the wheelchair. "Some students will do ANYTHING to get out of going to class."

Danielle laughed and some of Claire's tension dissipated. Danielle was okay, she repeated to herself. She'd been in a minor accident. She hadn't tried to hurt herself again.

"Are you kidding?" Danielle asked. "Your class is my favorite."

"Well, we'll see how you feel after you finish that first test next week."

"I'm going to ace it. Especially now that I get to miss therapy and yoga. I get to miss yoga, Mom," Danielle said.

"Yes, you do. For at least two weeks."

"That's like three hours a day I can spend studying."

"Probably more like three extra hours a day to sleep," Grayson teased.

Danielle yawned. "Good idea."

Once they got back home and got Danielle into her bed, Claire walked back downstairs with Grayson.

"That pain medicine knocked her out," Claire said.

"It's good for her to get some sleep."

"Is it going to be very painful?"

"Hard to say. It depends on the swelling."

They reached the front door. "I'll come by tomorrow after class to check on her."

"Okay," she said as he pulled her against him into a close hug. They stood hugging as the minutes ticked past. When the grandfather clock in the foyer tolled the midnight hour, Grayson pulled back. "I'll see you tomorrow," he said and slipped out the door.

Claire locked the door and leaned against it.

It was only a hug.

But it had been like coming home.

6

*G*rayson stood in the middle of the supermarket riddled with indecisiveness. What did one give an 18-year-old college student as a get-well gift? As a college professor, he needed to know these things. Too late, he realized he should have asked the student worker in the office.

He went up to the customer service counter and asked the young girl working there. "What kind of gift do you recommend to give a college student who's recovering from an accident?"

"It depends on what she likes."

"I don't know her all that well," he said.

The girl raised her eyebrows. "A flower?"

"She's my girlfriend's daughter," he clarified.

"What does she like?"

"All I know is she's a college student. Oh. And she has a kitten."

"Some cat toys? And an Amazon gift card?"

"Perfect!" He said. He located the pet aisle and started with a round blue pet bed. He put in some stuffed rats and a collapsible wand with something shiny on the end. He threw in a couple cans of canned cat food and moved to the gift card section. He picked a one-hundred-dollar amazon gift card.

Satisfied with his selections for Danielle, he started toward the checkout, passing the florist on his way. Going with impulse, he chose a single get well balloon and had blown up for purchase. The florist rang up his purchase and helped him arrange the cat toys with the gift card sitting in the middle, wrapped it with cellophane and tied it with bright blue ribbons to match the balloon.

Pleased with his purchase, Grayson took it out to the car and drove the short distance to Claire's house. He was getting used to the area and didn't feel quite so intimidated anymore. He noticed that one of Claire's neighbors needed to clean his gutters and another had a foot-high ant hill encroaching on his sidewalk.

The people may have bigger, nicer houses, but they still had the same problems as everyone else.

Claire met him at the door with her phone to her ear. "Sorry," she mouthed.

"For Danielle," he said, indicating the cat bed.

Claire put her hand over her phone. "She's in the living room." She walked toward the kitchen. "Surely we can reschedule," he heard her saying.

"Hi there," Grayson said, stopping at the living room door. Danielle was sitting on the sofa with her arm in a sling and a pained look on her face. Charlie was on his back swatting the fringe on the throw. "I brought you and Charlie something."

He set the package on the sofa next to her.

"You can sit," she said.

"How's your shoulder?"

"It hurts," she said. "What did I miss today?"

"Nothing," he said, holding out his phone. "I recorded it for you."

"Seriously!"

"Yeah, let's keep it between us, okay?"

"Sure."

He handed her his phone. "You can send it to yourself," he said.

She took his phone and a couple of seconds later, hers chimed. "Thank you." She tore the cellophane off and snagged the gift card, putting it on the end table next to her before unwrapping the collapsible pole with the shiny thing on the end of it.

She bobbed it in front of Charlie and he went wild chasing it wherever Danielle swung it.

She giggled and Grayson laughed.

"What are you two up to?" Claire asked, coming into the room.

"Look, Mom. Grayson brought toys for Charlie."

"I see," she said, turning a warm gaze in Grayson's direction. "How thoughtful."

"What's going on?" he asked.

"Danielle, would you like some tea?"

"Sure," Danielle said, giggling at Charlie's antics.

"Let's get some tea," Claire said, motioning for Grayson to follow her. They went into the kitchen and Claire turned on the teakettle.

"I love it that I can be here with her, but I had a major committee meeting set up for tomorrow. It's going to take some work to get everything rescheduled."

"Then don't," he said. "I can stay with her."

"It's likely to go late into the evening."

"All the more reason for me to be here."

She pressed her fingertips against her forehead. "Really? No," She turned off the tea kettle. "I can't ask you to babysit."

"Claire," he said. "She's not a baby. And you didn't ask. I like Danielle. We can hang out and watch movies."

She poured water into three mugs. He smiled when she didn't even ask him if he wanted any.

"Okay," she said. "Are you sure it's not an inconvenience?"

"I wouldn't offer if it was."

She stirred and turned to him.

"I know you're a package deal now," he said. "I'm good with that. I actually like it. You and Danielle need my help. Let me help you."

"Okay," she said. "Can you grab one of these?"

He picked up two mugs and they carried them into the living room.

"I need to call Martie," Claire said, leaving them.

"Sure."

"Can you stay?" Danielle asked. "Mom and I are going to watch *The 100*."

Grayson grinned. "If you Mom says it's okay."

"Are you kidding," Danielle said. "Mom's crushing on you."

Grayson sat on the other end of the sofa and grinned. "Seriously?"

Danielle laughed. "You two are like teenagers."

When Claire got off the phone and joined them, they ordered Chinese take-out and binge watched *The 100*. Claire pulled a footstool up and sat between them in the middle of the sofa. She slipped her feet out of her sneakers and propped her bare feet on the stool. Grayson followed suit and pulled off his shoes. He propped his feet, with his white socks, on the foot stool. He was distracted the whole time they were watching TV by his feet being only inches from hers.

Geez. He had to remind himself that they weren't teenagers anymore. He was quite content to just sit next to her, their feet almost touching.

Though he was enjoying their time together, he was looking forward to saying goodnight.

After she noticed Danielle falling asleep, she suggested she go to bed. She followed Danielle up to bed to help her put on her pajamas. Then she came back downstairs to tell Grayson goodnight.

He'd been answering emails on his phone. Students were starting to stress now that their first test was coming up.

"I'm glad you stayed," Claire said.

"Thanks for letting me. I had a blast."

"You're sure about tomorrow?" she asked.

"Stop asking. I'm looking forward to it. You don't mind if I cook in your kitchen, do you?"

"Of course not. Enjoy yourself."

He rubbed his hands together. "Danielle's vegetarian, too, right?"

"As far as I know."

"That's okay. I have some vegetarian tricks up my sleeve."

He pulled her into a hug. She started to pull away, but he pulled her closer.

He didn't want to let her go. Ever.

But this time when she pulled away, he kissed her on the forehead and squeezed her hands. "I'll see you tomorrow," he said.

CLAIRE WAS happy she could make the committee meeting, but she wanted to be somewhere else. She wanted to be home, with Danielle and Grayson. They were there in her kitchen. Without her.

She clicked on her phone to check the time again. They were interviewing mentors today. She should have delegated it. But she liked to keep a tight rein on her company.

Old habits were hard to break. If she was going to start having some semblance of a personal life, she had to become more comfortable at delegating.

Her mind was wandering anyway.

She kept thinking about being in Grayson's arms. The feel of his lips on her forehead. Wanted more. So much more.

"Do you want stir-fry or spaghetti?" Grayson asked, putting the sacks of groceries on the counter. "I brought stuff to make both."

"Spaghetti," Danielle said. She sat at the breakfast table nook, with her headphones on listening to her lectures. She hit pause. "It's really hard to keep up when you're not there sitting in the classroom."

"I agree," he said. "That's why I refuse to teach online classes. I took an online class once. And it was a joke. I learned absolutely nothing."

"I should be able to go back to class Monday," she said.

"Three days from now." He nodded. That should do it. "You would have only missed two days. Not bad. Only a week's worth of material during the regular semester. But," he stopped and waited until she looked up. "You can only come to class if you let your mother drive you."

Danielle scoffed. "That's not a problem. I'm not one of those people who thinks if you don't drive, you aren't grown up. I can be grown up and not drive. In fact, I think I'll move to New York when I get out of school so I never have to drive."

"Where did you get that idea? It's almost un-American."

She laughed. "Savannah talks about New York and how she wants to live there."

"Who's Savannah?"

"That's Daddy's wife."

It took Grayson a minute for his mind to wind its way around that piece of information. So, Claire's ex-husband had already remarried.

"Well, in that case, you can come to class on Monday."

She smiled and put her earbuds back in her ears.

Grayson chopped onions, bell peppers, and black olives. He found a large stove top pot and mixed in whole tomatoes, tomato paste, tomato sauce, three cans of cream of onion soup. He added the onions, bell peppers, black olives, and a host of Italian spices. After it simmered for awhile, he added in some grated parmesan cheese. While it simmered some more, he grated some mozzarella and poured some red wine into the pot.

He heated water in another pot for the pasta.

While he waited, he opened his MacBook and answered emails from students. He enjoyed the peacefulness of the kitchen, Danielle engrossed in her studies at the kitchen table, the view of the backyard, shaded by trees.

And more than anything, the knowledge that Claire would be home soon. He glanced up at the painting that she'd chosen, and that he'd bought and hung. His contribution to the house.

Charlie came into the room, sat in the middle of the kitchen floor, and started to meow.

He looked at Danielle. She took out her headphones. "He's hungry," she said.

"What do we feed him?" he asked.

She started to get up. Winced and sat back down. "It's in the pantry. There," she pointed, holding her shoulder. "There are little plates there, too, for him."

Grayson opened the cabinet and took out a can of kitten food and a plate. He dumped the food into the bowl and set it in the floor.

Charlie howled.

Danielle laughed. "You have to mash it up and put warm water on it."

Grayson did as she said and put the plate back in the floor. Charlie stopped meowing and lapped up the food.

There. Crisis solved. Now they could get back to their peaceful evening. He laughed at himself. He even liked the cat.

He turned everything off on the stove to wait for Claire and went back to his emails.

The doorbell rang. He and Danielle looked at each other. She shrugged.

"Want me to go see who it is?" he asked.

"Sure. I'm not expecting anyone."

Grayson went to the front of the house and opened the front door. A man, about his size, stood with his back to the door, one hand on the front porch post. Though he turned with a smile on his face, his smile quickly turned to confusion.

"Can I help you?" Grayson asked.

"I'm Noah."

Noah. Noah Worthington?

Danielle's father. Claire's ex-husband.

The pieces fell into place as the two men stood looking at each other. Grayson had a definite advantage. "I'm Grayson," he said. "Claire's... friend." He held out his hand.

Noah shook his hand, though he watched him warily.

"Come in," Grayson said, stepping back. "We're in the kitchen."

Noah followed him through the house.

Danielle looked up and saw Noah following him. "Daddy!" She said, standing up, wincing in pain.

Noah came across the room and hugged her gently. Then he stepped back and examined her sling. "Does it hurt?"

"Not so much," she said. "Only when I move it."

"I'm so glad you're okay, Baby," he said.

"Mom and Grayson are taking good care of me," she said.

"Grayson."

"Grayson is Mom's friend from high school," Danielle said.

"We met," Noah said. "Where's Claire?"

"She had a meeting," Danielle said. "We're going to eat when she gets home."

Danielle's phone chimed. "She'll be here in ten minutes."

Noah glanced at Grayson. Neither one said anything.

Danielle shoved her books aside.

Grayson put the angel hair on to cook. "Three minutes to dinner," he said to no one in particular. "We have plenty Noah. Can I get you something to drink?"

"Sure. But I can get it."

"No problem."

Noah poured a glass of wine for himself. "Want some?" he asked Grayson.

Grayson declined. Noah sat at the kitchen table next to Danielle.

While father and daughter talked, Grayson heated the sauce and drained the noodles. He set out plates and silverware on the counter. Everything was ready, but Claire would have to take it from here.

A few minutes later, Claire came into the room. "I'm home," she said, brightly.

"Hi Mom," Danielle said. "Noah's here."

Claire's expression went blank. Grayson wondered if Noah had a habit of making surprise visits.

"I see," she said. "Hello Noah."

Grayson watched their interaction. It was stiff. He wondered if it was because he was there. "Look," Grayson said, "Everything is ready for dinner," he said. "I can take off. Give you guys some privacy."

"No!" Danielle said.

"Don't even think about it," Claire said. "That's not even an option."

"I don't mind, really," Grayson said.

"I'm the one who should be leaving," Noah said. "I shouldn't have popped in uninvited. I didn't know…"

He didn't know anything had changed with Claire, Grayson thought.

"No one is leaving. Both of you are being silly," Claire said.

"Let's eat at the table. Noah, you set the table while Grayson and I get everything ready."

Noah took the plates and silverware to the dining room.

"I am so sorry," Claire whispered to Grayson. "He just does that. He just shows up without calling."

"It's okay," Grayson said. "I understand. He's Danielle's father."

"Still," she chewed her bottom lip. "I don't want you to feel awkward."

"I don't," he said, taking her hand. "Claire," he said, sweeping a strand of hair off her cheek. "I don't expect everything to change just because I'm here. I know you and Danielle have a life. I'm just grateful you let me be a little part of it."

Her chin trembled. "Thank you," she said. Then she seemed to shake it off and smiled. "This pasta smells delicious. I can't wait to try it."

"But…" he said. "There is one thing."

"What is it?" she asked. He heard the little catch in her voice.

"I promise to never show up unexpectedly."

He heard the relief in her laugh.

CLAIRE WAS NEARLY UNDONE. Her ex-husband and her high school sweetheart were here in her home at the same time. Having dinner.

And same said high school sweetheart was the guy she was currently crushing on.

She had to get herself in check. This would not do.

She'd nearly cried in front of Grayson.

Claire never did that.

Always in control.

It's what she had been taught. She was good at it.

But somehow all bets seemed to be off where Grayson was concerned.

Danielle seemed to be unaffected. Her father and her mother's guy friend over at the same time.

Maybe Danielle was unaffected because she had friends with unusual dynamics. Claire and Noah had been married longer than any of Danielle's friends' parents.

That was it, she decided. She took a deep breath and focused on enjoying the pasta Grayson had cooked for her and Danielle.

She was a little surprised that Noah had stayed. *Am I supposed to get used to this?* Would Noah be bringing his wife next time?

She shrugged. Stranger things had happened.

He loved Danielle beyond anything else. It was very important that she do everything she could to keep them all connected.

Besides she and Noah were going to be better as friends. Already, she could tell. She liked that there were no expectations when she saw him. No pretending required. And really, their relationship was the same now as it had pretty much ever been.

Seeing him didn't cause her heart rate to quicken the way it did when she saw Grayson. When she'd walked into her kitchen and saw both of them there, Noah sitting with Danielle and Grayson standing over the stove, she had been drawn to Grayson. Hands down.

She'd loved Noah. He was the father of her daughter and he was a good man. But she was... had been... in love with Grayson.

She carefully set down her glass of sparkling water and straightened the napkin in her lap.

She would have to think more about this. Later.

Right now she needed to keep her edge. Danielle was telling

Noah about her classes. Specifically, how much she loved her psychology class.

Grayson beamed.

"Honey, tell them about what you're taking this Fall," Claire said.

She rested her chin on her hands and watched her daughter interact with the men at her table. Just as she had thought earlier, Danielle seemed to have no problem with both of them being there. It was a most interesting situation.

Perhaps Danielle wouldn't mind having two fathers.

She pulled herself out of her fantasy world.

Grayson would be leaving soon, so that was just that. A fantasy.

But Claire had schooled herself well on living in the present.

And she suddenly realized that she, just as Danielle, honestly didn't mind having both of the men there at the same time.

"What do you do?" Noah asked Grayson.

"I'm a professor of psychology."

"He just retired from the Air Force," Danielle added.

"The Air Force?" Noah seemed surprised. "What did you do?"

"Pararescue."

"You jumped out of a few good planes," Noah said.

"Quite a few," Grayson said. "Do you parachute?"

"Oh no. My goal is keep the plane in the air, land smoothly, then step onto the ground."

The men laughed. "A good goal to have," Grayson agreed.

"My wife," Noah started, then stopped, glanced at Claire.

Claire shrugged.

"My wife, Savannah," Noah continued. "would love to talk to you. She's studying psychology and she's especially interested in studying traumatic experiences."

"I know quite a few men who went through them," Grayson said, easily, but Claire noticed the tension in his face. He took another bite, then set his fork down.

Danielle must have noticed, too. "Hey Dad," she said. "Did you know that we have something called mirror neurons?"

"What's a mirror neuron?" Noah asked.

"We have neurons in our brains that are activated when we watch someone feel something. So, when we see someone cry, our similar neurons are activated and we feel empathy for them. We essentially feel what they feel." She glanced at Grayson. He gave her a quick nod.

"That sounds neat, honey. Sounds like you're learning a lot."

"I am! Grayson has been teaching us all about biology and how the brain and body are connected."

"I'm proud of you, Danielle," Noah said.

"Your daughter is doing really well in class," Grayson said.

"I guess I'll know after my test next week," Danielle said. "It's a lot of material."

"I always say that intro psychology is the hardest psychology class," Grayson said. "You have to learn a little bit about all the different fields of psychology. There's a whole class on physiological psychology and you have to learn about the basics all in one chapter. Then you have to learn about the history of psychology and one on psychological disorders. You get a glimpse of everything and have to learn new terminology about everything."

"Even statistics," Danielle said.

"It sounds rigorous," Noah said.

"It is," Grayson agreed. "As long as she puts in the work, she'll be okay."

7

*A*fter dinner, Noah and Danielle went into the living room to "hang out," as Danielle put it. Grayson and Claire hung back to clean up and do the dishes.

Grayson was feeling a bit restless. "I'm gonna head out," he said.

"What? Why?" Claire said.

"It's late and I've been here since early afternoon. I've to get home and start making a test for next week."

"It's because Noah is here," Claire said.

"Sort of," he admitted as he put plates in the dishwasher. "But not in a bad way. I just met him, so I need to give you guys some time to adjust. I'll stay longer next time."

She stood holding the dishcloth, her mouth curved in that lovely little smile that he loved. "Okay," she said. "But next time, I do the cooking."

He took a step toward her. Took her hand and kissed her palm. "Or… maybe I'll take you out to dinner next time."

She smiled. "Sounds even better," she said.

"I'll say goodbye, then head out," he said.

She nodded. Then turned back to wipe at the counter. Everything was back in its place. It was as though he'd never been there.

He said goodbye to Danielle and Noah before slipping out the front door and bounding down the stairs to his car.

He sat for a minute, watching the house. He hadn't been completely truthful with Claire. It was hard to be there with Noah. Knowing that, even though they were divorced, Noah belonged there more than Grayson did.

Noah and Claire had a history. And they would have a reason to stay in touch. Danielle.

Grayson could deal with that. He liked Noah. Noah seemed like a good guy.

Grayson knew himself well enough to know what had gotten under his skin. It was talking about, even briefly, his time overseas. It only took a comment or a random reference to put his mind back there. And he used a lot of energy to keep that from happening.

He started up the motor and headed to his place. He did need to work on putting together the psychology exam for next week. But he also needed some time alone. Some time to settle himself.

Grayson fell asleep on the couch watching reruns of *Game of Thrones*.

Some time later, after being jarred awake, he knocked his phone on the floor as he grabbed for it.

He didn't recognize the number and didn't even know what time it was. He swiped to answer.

"Grayson?" The woman's voice was upset.

"Yes," Grayson sat up. A flash of fear shot through him. He hadn't spoken to either his mother or his sister lately. He pulled the phone away to glance at the unknown area code.

"This is Alex Taylor."

Grayson rubbed at his eyes. He didn't recognize the name. He squeezed the phone waiting for her to go on.

"I'm calling about my brother, Timothy. I don't know where his phone is, but he had me save your number in case I ever needed anything. I'm sorry to call so late."

Timothy Taylor. His best friend. "Is he okay?" Even as he said the words, he knew she wouldn't be calling if everything was okay.

"No," Alex said and her voice broke. "They took him to the emergency room. It's bad."

"What happened?" Grayson was awake now, but he couldn't process what she was saying. He'd just talked to Timothy, what, two weeks ago. Maybe three.

He'd gotten a new job and was about to be granted visitation to see his kids again.

"He shot himself." He heard her sobs through the phone line.

"What? When?"

"I don't know," she sobbed. "It was earlier today or last night. I don't know. I talked to him yesterday. He sounded kinda weird, so I came over to check on him this evening when he didn't answer his phone. The cops just left."

"Are you at his house?" he asked.

"I'm on my way to the hospital."

"Do you need me to come?" he asked.

"Would you? There's nobody but us. I don't know what to do."

"Okay. I'll see when I can get a flight to Houston and call you back. Is this your cell phone?"

"Yes," Alex said. "Thank you."

"Call me if you know anything."

He hung up the phone. And sat staring at it while he tried to process what he had to do. Timothy and he had a pact. They'd agreed to take care of each other's families if anything ever happened. They had also agreed to call each other if things ever got so bad they couldn't deal with it.

Then a memory stabbed him in the gut. Timothy had sent him a text last week. Grayson had been in the middle of class. Grayson scrolled back through his texts. Last Tuesday. *Call me when you get a minute.*

Grayson hadn't responded.

It wasn't Timothy who had broken the agreement. It was Grayson.

The guilt stabbed him like a knife. He had to get to Alex. He had to be there for Timothy. It was 9:45. He had to get online and find a flight. He had to pack.

He had to call Claire before it was too late.

He dialed her number before he changed his mind and before it got any later.

"Hello," she answered.

"Claire. Are you still awake?"

"Yeah. I'm just reading."

"I have to get to Houston," he blurted.

"Why?"

"My best friend's in the hospital. He attempted suicide and his sister called me." Grayson stood up and went toward his bedroom. He dragged his suitcase from the closet.

"When are you leaving?"

"I don't know. I've got to see when the first flight out is. I called you first."

"You need to leave now?"

"Yeah. They just took him to the ER. His sister is all alone."

"Hold on," she said. "Let me call you right back." The phone went dead in his ear.

Grayson tossed his phone on the bed along with his suitcase. He opened his iPad and looked up flights out of L.A.

Claire called back. "Can you be at the airport in two hours?" she asked.

"I think so." It was thirty minutes to the airport. That was about an hour to pack. He could do it in thirty.

"I'm going to text you a phone number. After you park your car at the airport call this number. Noah will take you to Houston in his plane."

"No," he said. "I can't let him do that."

"Of course, you can. It'll be impossible for you to get out tonight. Noah can have you there in no time."

"I couldn't ask…"

"You didn't. I did. And don't try to pay him."

"It's not about the money." He said. How could explain that it was more about how he felt about Claire?

"Then go pack. I'll text you the number. Call me in the morning when you know something about your friend."

"Okay," he said.

"I'll be here when you get back. Good night, Grayson," she said.

"Good night."

Before he could say anything else, she hung up the phone.

Grayson went into the bathroom and washed his face. This was a side of Claire he didn't know. Calm and decisive. He liked it.

While he was in the bathroom, he tossed his toiletries into his shaving kit and carried it back to his suitcase.

Timothy better pull out of this, Grayson thought. Because *you owe me one, buddy.*

"Noah, are you sure you don't mind?" Claire asked.

"I was heading that way in the morning anyway," he said, as he locked in the flight on his iPad.

"But you haven't slept."

"I'll get a room in Houston and sleep before I head up to Ft. Worth tomorrow."

"Thank you," she said.

"Thanks for coming to check on me," Danielle said.

"I'm just glad you're okay, kitten," he said.

"When can you come back?" Danielle asked.

"When do you want me to?" he asked.

Danielle scoffed. "Tomorrow."

Noah kissed Danielle on the top of her head. "You know I would," he said. "How about if I call you tomorrow." He glanced at Claire. "I guess I'd better start calling before I show up."

Claire laughed. "Then you wouldn't be you."

"Sometimes that wouldn't be a bad thing."

"I'll walk you to the door," Claire said.

"Danielle said you know Grayson from high school," Noah said when they were out of earshot of their daughter.

"We dated," she said.

"And now?"

"I don't know. Nothing can come of it."

"Why not? You seem to have a good thing."

"He's moving away in a couple of months."

"That's too bad," he said. "He seems like good guy."

"He is."

"And you like him."

Claire smiled and realized that, yes, she did like him. Even after all this time. She'd never stopped liking him.

"Maybe you can change his mind," he said.

Claire shook her head. "I don't think so."

"There's always hope," he said. "Look at me."

Noah was the eternal optimist. Especially since he'd gotten back together with Savannah. They had been college sweethearts. Ever since they'd gotten back together, Noah had been an insufferably happy romantic.

He swept his thumb under her chin. "I'll take good care of him," he said.

Claire had learned a lot about Noah when they'd gone

through therapy after Danielle's suicide attempt. She learned that he'd never gotten over Savannah.

Claire, however, had never mentioned Grayson. In fact, she'd managed to talk about herself as little as possible. She'd only talked about work and, as a result, Noah had learned something about her.

They'd come out of Danielle's crisis with a new respect for each other and a friendship they'd never had before. She liked that they were no longer at odds.

After Noah left, Claire curled up on the sofa with Danielle and they watched the Hunger Games together until Danielle started to fall asleep.

"Come on, Sweetheart, let's go to bed."

Danielle stood up and winced.

"Do you need some medication?" Claire asked.

Danielle shook her head. "I have to get up tomorrow and study. It makes me sleep too much."

Claire helped Danielle change into her pajamas and tucked her into bed.

She went to her computer and began putting together an ad seeking her next artist. It was her tried and true method of dealing with emotions.

GRAYSON DIDN'T MAKE it in time. When he got to the ER and asked for Timothy, the nurse had pointed him toward a woman curled up in the corner, sobbing.

"Alex?" he said, going up to her.

She lifted her face, her eyes swollen. She nodded. And began wailing.

"Hey," Grayson said, kneeling next to her and taking the woman he'd never met, the sister of his best friend, in his arms.

When she finally quieted, heavy in his arms, he wondered if

she'd passed out. "Hey," he said, nudging her gently. "I'm gonna get you some water and a cloth for your face."

He shifted her to rest her head on a chair. Grayson escaped and went straight to the nurse's station. He asked for water and a wash cloth. And information.

Timothy had died about an hour ago from a self-inflicted gunshot wound.

"We need to contact the VA." he said.

"We'll take care of it, sir," she said.

He took the water back to Alex. She was sitting up now. He handed her the wet wash cloth, but she just held it. He took it back from her and washed her face.

"What do I do now?" she asked, her voice hoarse.

"I'll take care of it," he said. "Is there someone I can call for you?"

She looked into his eyes and the tears started again. "There's no one," she said. "Just you."

Grayson sat next to Alex and put his elbows on his knees. His friend Timothy had given twenty years of his life for his country. He was a decorated veteran with no one to grieve for him except his sister and his best friend.

Now he was a statistic. One of the many who fell victim to suicide.

Grayson had slept a little on the three-hour flight to Houston, but he was emotionally drained.

How had things gotten so bad with Timothy? How had they gotten so bad that he'd chosen a permanent solution to a temporary problem?

Grayson knew there were far too many similarities between himself and Timothy. Grayson, too, had no family other than his mother and sister. The parallels sent a shiver down his back.

What would he do if he found himself Timothy's shoes? May God protect him from that.

Grayson did not want to spend the rest of his life alone.

With no one to call if he fell into the depths of despair.

With no children to keep him alive. Children were the number one protective factor against completed suicide.

Grayson had never given much thought to having children. Not since Claire.

Perhaps it time to think about it again.

CLAIRE HAD RECEIVED ONLY three messages from Grayson since he'd left in the middle of the night Friday. One was as he'd promised saying he'd arrived safely. The second was that his friend had died. And the third was that he would let her know when he was headed back. All three messages had come through at various times of the day Saturday.

It was Thursday and he still hadn't contacted her again. She couldn't help wondering what he'd gotten into. Danielle said that their test had been postponed and someone else had been teaching their class for 4 days now. Danielle was not happy. She said all they did was take notes and she missed Grayson's entertaining teaching style and examples.

Patience was the one thing Claire was good at. Noah had unintentionally schooled her well in that. She'd basically learned to see him when she saw him.

If she and Grayson had been in a relationship, she told herself, she would have called him. No more waiting and wondering.

But they weren't in a relationship. And they weren't going to be. Less than two months and he would be on his way. It wasn't wise to get too attached.

Reattached.

Claire turned off her computer and stood up. She stretched and checked the time. It was time to meet Danielle for lunch. Then counseling.

She checked her phone. No messages.

She grabbed her handbag and, as she walked through the gallery, glanced at the two new paintings that had come in for her review.

Neither one particularly drew her to them. Not enough to bring the artist in.

She would put out another ad.

Danielle didn't have much to say at lunch. After four days of not having Grayson teaching her psychology class, her interest in the subject had waned. They both spent much of their time at lunch on their phones.

After lunch, they got into the car to drive to the mental health clinic.

"Do you want to drive?" Claire asked.

Danielle lifted her shoulder in its sling.

"I know," Claire said. "But do you want to? It's been ages since you've asked to drive. You should be used to your antidepressants by now."

"No," Danielle said, scrunching her nose.

"I thought all teenagers wanted to drive."

"Driving is retro. I'm gonna have a driver when I go to work."

Claire laughed. "Really? How are you going to afford this driver?

Danielle shrugged and resumed texting. "I don't know. I'll probably just live close to work and walk."

Claire moved into traffic and considered her daughter's statement. Danielle's father had the same aversion to driving. Perhaps Danielle inherited this from Noah. In Noah, it manifested in wanting to fly everywhere. Danielle didn't want to fly, but she didn't want to drive either. Her daughter preferred to keep her eyes glued to her phone.

Generations were changing, Claire mused.

Her phone chimed indicating a text message. Claire's hand

reflexively moved to pick up her phone. She glanced at her daughter and put her hand back on the wheel.

And sighed.

Perhaps she couldn't blame Noah after all. Perhaps Danielle was just a product of her time. Maybe, Claire thought, she should get a driver.

Her fingers itched to check her message, but she made it all the way to the mental health parking lot before she grabbed her phone.

It was text from Grayson. *I'm back in town. Catching up. Teaching tomorrow. Dinner tomorrow night?*

She followed Danielle into the clinic with a little spring in her step that had been missing all week. They sat in the waiting area and Claire sent back a quick text. *Okay.*

She didn't want to seem overly enthusiastic, but the smile on her face had Danielle looking at her sideways.

"You heard from Grayson." Danielle said.

Claire bit her lip to hide the smile that threatened to spread across her face.

"You did!" Danielle said. "Is he back?"

"He'll be in class tomorrow."

"Thank goodness," Danielle said. "I don't think I could stand another day of those boring lectures."

"You do know, that most college professors do just that – lecture?"

"Danielle?" Dr. Lee called from his office door.

Claire and Danielle went into his office and settled onto Dr. Lee's couch. He sat across from them and smiled. "You both look rather happy today."

"Mom's crushing on my psychology professor," Danielle said.

"Danielle," Claire said, her cheeks hot. "I am not!"

"Well, technically he's her old boyfriend from high school, but they haven't seen each other for like twenty years."

Dr. Lee studied Claire. Smiled. "I've never seen you look this happy," he said.

"Things are going well," she said. "At the foundation."

Dr. Lee glanced at Danielle who shrugged. "It's okay," he said, turning back to Claire. "to have some happiness in your life."

"I have happiness," she said.

"Good," Dr. Lee said, then turned back to Danielle. "What's going on with you, Danielle?"

As Danielle talked about her classes and her new boyfriend - that Claire hadn't known about - Claire, reflected about what Dr. Lee had said.

Did people really think she wasn't happy? Was she happy? Had she ever been happy?

She was happy. They had been right, she did have to admit. She was crushing on her old boyfriend. And...

Claire realized she had been happy in high school, her sophomore and junior year before Grayson left for the Air Force. In fact, her fondest memories were there. With him.

History, it seemed, was repeating itself.

In more ways than one. She'd known then that he would be leaving for the military. And she knew now that he was leaving for a one year teaching position. He'd said he was coming back then. This time he hadn't said that.

This time he wasn't making any promises.

We're not in a relationship this time.

"Claire, are you alright?" Dr. Lee asked.

Claire jerked herself out of her reverie and smiled. "Yes. I'm good."

"Danielle was just asking if she could have her guy friend come over tomorrow."

Claire looked at Danielle who was watching her expectantly. "Of course. She doesn't have to ask me that."

"You'll have to go pick him up, Mom. He lives on campus and he doesn't have a car."

"Do you want to go get him?" Claire asked.

Danielle held up her bum shoulder.

"Right. Of course. I'll drive you to pick him up." So tomorrow, Claire contemplated, she would be double-dating with her daughter.

8

$\mathcal{T}$he rain set in the next day. The weather channel described it as a rare westward monsoon thunderstorm.

Grayson juggled his umbrella, three pizza boxes, and a single red rose he'd picked up for Claire. It would have been a perfect day to get delivery, but Claire wanted to try a new pizza place that didn't deliver.

Grayson didn't mind picking up the pizza. He just needed to find a way to keep everything from getting soaked.

When he got to the safety of the front porch he was soaked, but somehow he'd managed to keep the pizza and the flower dry. Mission accomplished.

Claire opened the door and burst out laughing.

"I'm sorry," she said, biting her lip. "It's not funny. You're soaked."

"I'm glad I could provide humor to your day," he said.

She took the pizza from him and set it on the table in the foyer. He took the rose from under his jacket and handed it to her. A host of emotions ran across her face, the strongest being surprise.

"Oh. Wow," she said, closing her eyes as she inhaled its scent.

He didn't ask. Didn't want to know. But he could only imagine that it had been quite some time since anyone thought to bring her a flower. Even something so simple as a rose bud.

When she opened her eyes, she had so much unguarded emotion, it caught him off guard. "You're beautiful," he said.

Again, surprise.

And he felt so much regret for the girl he'd left behind all those years ago.

If he knew then what he knew now, he would have found another career. He would have found a way to stay with Claire.

He vowed to himself in that moment to do everything he could to make it up to her.

"Is Claire's boyfriend here?" he asked.

"They're in the living room playing a video game. Thank you for getting the pizza. If I'd known it was going to rain, we would've gotten delivery instead."

"I don't mind the rain," he said. "And anything for two beautiful girls."

"You're soaked," she said.

"Yeah," he ran a hand along his jeans. He'd gotten wet getting the pizza, then again getting from his car to Claire's door.

"Let me put those in the dryer for you."

"I don't have any other clothes."

"Some of Noah's are still upstairs in a box. I'll grab you some sweats and a t-shirt," she said and before he could answer, she dashed upstairs. About two minutes later, she was back.

"You can change in the bathroom right here," she said, indicating the half-bath on the way to the kitchen.

Grayson took the clothes into the bathroom and after drying off with a towel, pulled on the sweatpants and shirt. He refused to give any more thought about wearing her ex-husband's clothes.

After changing, he took the wet clothes and handed them to her. She put them in the dryer, then they took the pizza into the living room and Danielle introduced them to Joey.

"Joey's in our class," Danielle said.

"Sure," Grayson said, hoping he hid the fact that he had no idea. The college freshmen all looked alike to him. Until he got to know them, of course. It was one of those unfortunate things that went along with aging.

"Are you two ready for your test on Monday?" he asked.

They looked at each other. "We're going to go upstairs and study after we eat," Danielle said.

Claire rolled her eyes and looked at Grayson. "We did a lot of studying in our day, didn't we Grayson?"

Grayson was so caught off guard by her statement, it took him a minute, then he burst out laughing. "I blame our *studying* on that C I got in Calculus. But your mother was a different story. No matter how much we studied, she still managed to pull off A's every time."

Claire blushed. He had caught her by surprise, too, it seemed.

"You started it," he said, with a wink.

"Well, why don't we eat this pizza before it gets cold. Grayson had to brave the thunderstorm and rain to get it here."

The youngsters only needed one invitation.

After they ate, they were true to their word and headed off upstairs to study.

"Some things never change," he said.

"What? Their studying?" Claire asked as she stacked plates. "I much prefer them *studying* upstairs than being out somewhere doing drugs."

"That's an excellent point. And I agree completely."

"Hey," Claire said. "Have you noticed that young people

don't care about driving and cars anymore? Or is it just Danielle?"

"No. I've noticed. With a couple of exceptions, they don't go to malls either."

"I think it's because they aren't motivated to go anywhere. They can do everything on their phones."

"Almost everything," he said, teasingly, indicating the giggles coming from upstairs.

"It's been awhile…" she said.

"Since you've seen anyone?"

"Ha. There have only been two for me."

"Two? Two men?"

She kept her eyes down as she put the pizza boxes in the garbage disposal. "You. And then I married Noah. I've only been divorced for less than a year."

She straightened and raised her chin. Did he imagine the ever so slight quiver of her chin? "And you? Are you seeing anyone?"

"I like to think I'm seeing you," he said.

Her eyes widened and she turned away to wash her hands in the sink. With the dish cloth in her hands, she turned back to face him. "Are we doing this again?"

He was blindsided by her question. Were they? "No," he said. Her eyes widened. "Claire." He did the only thing he could think of to do. He closed the distance between them and drew her into a hug. She put her arms around him. And he just held her to him.

"I don't know how to answer that question," he said, murmuring against her ear.

"I know. You don't have to," she whispered.

"No. I think I do. It's only fair." He pulled back and took her hand. "Let's go sit, okay?"

They went into the living room and sat next to each other on the sofa. He held her hands in his. So soft.

"I didn't think I'd ever see you again," he said. "I thought you were happily married. So I left you alone."

She nodded and lowered her gaze. "It's okay."

"No," he said, lifting her chin until she met his gaze again. "I can't just bust in here and upend your life again. Not when I'm about to leave again. That isn't fair."

"Grayson…"

"No." He shook his head. "It's not fair to you. But the thing is, I can't help myself."

"So… what do we do?" She asked.

He let go of her hands and sat back, scrubbed at his face. "I have to go. I signed a one-year contract."

"I'm not asking you not to go."

"I know. I'm not saying that."

"What are you saying?"

"I'm not sure," he said. "I guess I'm saying that if we are doing this again, I'll do my part differently."

"You did everything right."

He scoffed. "No. I didn't. I was more focused on my career than staying in touch with you."

"Grayson, how can you say that? You wrote me all those letters and you called."

"All I had to do was get an email address."

"You didn't know. You were young."

"Still."

"Grayson," she said, sliding closer to him. "What my mother did was wrong. She knows that. We have to let go of the past."

He lifted his gaze to hers and put his fingers on her cheek. He ran his thumb along her bottom lip. Her lips parted.

"Claire," he said and put his lips on hers.

When Grayson's lips touched hers, it was like a lightning bolt shot through her body. Her lips remembered.

Her heart remembered.

The years disappeared and they were back in her parents' house, making out on the couch again.

Everything shifted and she knew nothing would be the same again.

It didn't matter that Grayson was leaving again.

Just like it hadn't mattered that he was leaving all those years ago. In fact, the knowledge that he was going away made it all the more sweet. All the more to be savored.

A warning went off in her head.

Was that why she'd slept with him before? Because she knew he would be leaving and she wouldn't have to deal with it?

No.

She shifted back and her eyes fluttered open.

"We can't," she uttered.

"I know," he said. "the kids."

"No. We can't," she said again, a little louder this time.

"I'm sorry," he said. "I thought…"

"I do." She shifted and stared at the fireplace. "It's different now. We aren't kids."

"And I'm leaving again," he said.

"Yeah," she said, turning back to him. "You're leaving again."

"We have two months," he said.

She shook her head. "No."

"Claire. Let me have another chance. Like you said, we aren't kids. We can talk every day. We can visit all the time. Until I can figure out something."

"I won't leave L.A." She'd left L.A. once before. Her home was here. Her dream home. That she had designed from the ground up. Her business was here. Her contacts. The only time she'd been unable to visit was when she had been pregnant with Danielle. She'd been miserable and had redoubled her efforts to establish her business here. She was an L.A. girl.

Through and through. "You have to know that up front," she said.

"Fair enough. I understand."

"And I won't sleep with you until... well... until... it's right."

He laughed. "That's not what I'm after. I mean, it is, but it's not all I'm after. I enjoy you, Claire. Just being with you.

"No pressure, then?"

"None. The opposite of pressure." He held up his hands.

She laughed, glad to have the tension broken. "What's the opposite of pressure?"

"I'm not sure. We'll have to figure that out."

"That should be interesting," she said.

"We'll have the anti-pressure relationship," he agreed.

She looked at him for a minute. "What does that even look like?"

"I don't know. I think we'll have to invent it."

"Okay."

"Come here," he said, pulling her into a hug.

She tucked her head under his chin and pulled her feet onto the sofa and wrapped her arms around him. He smelled so good. Like soap and rainwater all mixed in together. It reminded her of the time they'd been caught in the rain on the Santa Monica beach. They were supposed to be at the library, studying. But it had been such a beautiful Sunday afternoon. One minute they were enjoying each other in the sunshine and the next, after ignoring the dark clouds and coming in just a little too late, they'd been running along the path to their car.

"Do you remember Santa Monica?" she asked.

"We laughed the whole way back to the car."

"I thought my mother was going to kill me when we came in the house drenched."

"You should have heard my father when I tried to explain about the mud inside his car," Grayson said.

"Oh," She shifted to look up at him. "You never told me."

"It was no big deal. I just cleaned it up and was grounded for a week," he said.

"Ah. That explains a lot."

"Yeah, well, I stayed grounded a lot."

"It was my fault," she said.

"Yes, it was." He squeezed her. "But I wouldn't have traded a single minute of it."

"I'm sorry to interrupt, but…" Joey said.

Claire jumped to a sitting position. "What is it Joey?"

"Danielle asked me to come get you."

"What's wrong?"

"She um… fell… off the bed," His face was beet red. "I think she might have hurt her shoulder."

Claire was up running up the stairs in a heartbeat with Grayson at her heels.

"Danielle?"

Danielle sat on the floor holding her arm. Claire knelt next to her. "We were playing with Charlie," she said. The kitten sat on the bed, innocently licking his paws.

"Where does it hurt?" Grayson asked, kneeling next to them.

"My shoulder."

"This is where you bumped it," Claire said.

"It's probably just bruised again," he said.

"I think I broke it."

"Can I look," Grayson asked, looking from Claire to Danielle.

Claire nodded. Danielle said "okay."

Grayson gently removed the sling and pressed his fingers against her shoulder.

She winced.

"I'm sorry," he said.

"It's okay," Danielle kept her chin high.

"It's not broken," Grayson said.

"Are you sure?" Danielle asked. "It hurts like a... hurts like crazy."

"Pararescue," Grayson said. "Remember?"

"Right."

"Okay, let's get you off the floor and up on the bed. Joey, will you help?"

Joey moved forward. "What do I do?"

"Just let her grab your arm. Never pull on her."

Danielle grabbed Joey's arm and with Grayson supporting her back, she got to her feet and back onto the bed.

"How did you get into pararescue?" Joey asked.

"I went into the Air Force," Grayson said.

"Awesome. And you jumped out of airplanes?"

"All the time."

"Maybe I should do that."

Grayson laughed, but locked his gaze onto Claire's. "Maybe you should see where this thing with Danielle is going first."

Danielle groaned. "We don't have a thing."

"We could have a thing," Joey said.

"Do you need anything, else, Danielle?" Claire asked. "Grayson and I are going to go back downstairs."

"No. I'm good. Thanks, Grayson."

"No problem."

Claire and Grayson left them discussing the possibility of *having a thing.*

Grayson grimaced. "I think I might have overstepped."

"No," Claire said. "Let them have that conversation. Maybe someone should have mentioned something to us."

"Yeah. We're the old wise ones now."

"Ha. It's an unknown hazard of parenting."

"And teaching."

"I imagine there are a lot of similarities."

"Except I get to leave them behind when I go home at night."

"That's when the fun starts," she said.

"Danielle likes baseball?"

"Yeah, how did you know?"

"Well, she has a poster of the Dodgers on her wall and a couple of baseballs on her dresser where most girls have Barbies."

"It's something she and her father used to do together."

"Used to."

"They still go, but not as often."

"That's too bad."

"It's okay. She's into college now. I should see if your clothes are dry."

"Is that a hint?"

She rolled her eyes. "I'll be right back."

Claire left Grayson in the living room and went to the laundry room. His clothes were dry. She looped his jeans and shirt over her arm and carried them back out to him. "You can wear what you have on home if you like."

Grayson chuckled. "You are telling me it's time to go."

"No. You can stay, but you'll see a grown woman fall asleep on the couch."

He smiled and ran a finger over her chin. "I'm tired, too. Are you busy tomorrow?"

"I have to take Danielle to visit my mom, then I'm free."

He ran his finger over her bottom lip.

She took a step back. "'Do you want to come with me?" she asked.

"Whoa. I don't know."

She smiled. "You have to face it some time. Better sooner than later, don't you think?"

"I don't know, Claire. Sometimes it's best to put off today what you can do tomorrow."

9

Grayson picked up his dry cleaning, dashed through the supermarket for basics like sodas and bread, then filled up his car with gas. Saturdays were for errands and getting everything ready for next week. The Air Force had taught him nothing if not discipline.

He didn't mind working hard. In fact, while other people were standing around complaining about not having enough time to do things, he was off doing them.

He subscribed to the work hard play hard club. He worked hard, then he tucked work away and played. He was good at compartmentalization.

Teaching college was turning out to be different, however, and he found it be taxing. His work was bleeding over into his play time. It was part of society's culture. Take the good with the bad, he mused.

Unfortunately, when a student emailed or texted, they expected an answer right away. Even on the weekends. And with their first test coming up on Monday, the questions were coming like wildfire. It hadn't helped that he'd been out nearly a whole week.

He stopped at Starbuck's for a coffee, sat outside, and while sipping his coffee, did a quick check-up of messages. Then he sat back and watched people for a few minutes. Some people were obviously heading to work, but most were like him. Running errands and starting their weekend off with a jolt of caffeine.

One couple, in their twenties, caught his attention. They were giggling with their heads bent close as they ordered and waited for their coffee. He couldn't help but wonder if he'd made the wrong decision by entering the Air Force like he did. Not that regretted his military service. He'd do that part all over again. Even knowing that he'd sometimes have nightmares and intrusive memories. Nothing four weeks in the VA hospital in Little Rock hadn't helped him get under control. But maybe he should have married Claire first. Their lives would have been different. He would have been gone, so she still could have had the career she had today. The only thing that would have changed was that they would had a life together. A family.

Grayson was still grieving the loss of his friend. But in truth, he was grieving more the tragedy than anything else. He knew the statistics. He knew that veterans took their lives everyday. Suicide wasn't just a military phenomenon, but these men and women had only been doing their jobs – serving their country. The resulting post-traumatic reaction was a travesty.

He tossed his empty cup in the trash and shook off his thoughts. He couldn't rewrite the past. Still, he couldn't help thinking that there should be more that he could do to help his fellow veterans.

Grayson had three hours before he was supposed to meet Claire at her house. Then the three of them were going to Claire's mother's house.

He could think of plenty of things he'd rather do than face Claire's mother. He hadn't done anything wrong. She was the one who had hidden his letters and phone calls from Claire. He could only imagine that he was the last person she wanted to see.

Arriving back at his apartment, he put away his dry cleaning and his groceries. He decided to change clothes again, opting for a white button-down shirt in place of the casual polo shirt he'd put on that morning.

With some time left, he turned on his computer and went to the veteran's administration website to look around. There were lots of social worker jobs, but no openings.

He came across one of his buddies from grad school, Bob. He and Bob had taken every class together.

He found Bob's email address and dashed off a quick email before heading out the door to pick up Claire.

They were waiting for him. They'd been sitting on the sofa playing Words with Friends back and forth.

Claire was cute in a mid-thigh length flared skirt, a t-shirt, cropped sweater, and white canvas sneakers. Danielle had on jeans and a sweatshirt.

Claire seemed a little nervous. He asked her about it.

"I didn't tell my mother you were coming. In fact, I haven't mentioned you since she gave me the letters."

"Oh. Well. That's comforting. Nothing like busting up on the one person who tried successfully to get rid of me."

"It wasn't you. She likes you. It was the lifestyle that scared her. She'll be fine now."

"Easy for you to say."

Danielle looked up from her phone. "You'll like Grandma," she said. "She's really a kind person. I've never heard her speak unkindly of anyone."

"That's comforting," Grayson said. "Thank you for telling me."

"No problem," Danielle said, putting her gaze back on her phone.

The twenty-minute ride to Betty Beauchamp's house was mostly silent. Danielle was texting. Grayson and Claire were lost in their own thoughts.

He parked at the curb and they walked up the sidewalk, Danielle in front.

Betty was waiting at the door. Danielle, according to Claire, was the one person who could lure her from her rooms upstairs without complaint.

Betty, Grayson, reflected, looked good physically, but there was a sadness about her.

They hugged and talked about Danielle's shoulder before Betty turned to Claire. Claire hugged her mother, then turned to Grayson.

"Mom," she said. "This is…"

Her mother interrupted. "Grayson." Smiling, she reached out and took his hands in hers. "It's so good to see you again."

"It's good to see you, too, Mrs. Beauchamp."

"Let's go inside, shall we? I made lunch."

"Are you sure she didn't know I was coming?" Grayson whispered as they followed Betty and Danielle into the house."

"I didn't tell her," Claire said.

"Danielle," Grayson said.

Claire shrugged. "Maybe."

Betty had made tuna sandwiches. They sat at the kitchen table eating tuna sandwiches and chips while Danielle chattered to her grandmother about her classes, her shoulder, and Joey.

After they ate, Betty and Danielle went out back to fill Betty's bird feeders.

"You'd never know they talked every day," Claire said.

"Really? Every day?"

"Yep."

"Nope. I thought it must have been at least a week."

Claire laughed. "The two of them are thick as thieves."

"Must be nice," he said. "To have someone that close."

"I never did."

"Yeah. Me either," he said.

"You never talked about your grandparents."

"Nothing to talk about. My grandfather was military, so they lived in Germany while I was growing up. I saw them maybe one time."

"That's unfortunate. What about on the other side?"

"Died before I could get to know them."

"Same thing on Noah's side. I mean his mother's still living, but they weren't close."

"Was Danielle close to your father?"

"She was. I think that's part of what led to her suicide attempt."

"She seems good now," Grayson said.

"She's great. At first, they said we should watch her when she was too happy, but now they agree that she really is okay."

"That must be a relief."

Claire blew her hair out of her eyes. "You have no idea," she said.

"You said she's spending the night?" he asked.

"Yeah. We have the rest of the day to ourselves."

He grinned. "That sounds irresistible."

She raised a delicate eyebrow.

"Actually," he said. "I was thinking. The Getty is having an art exhibit that you might like if you haven't seen it. It's 18th Century Europe."

"Ooh. I haven't seen it. But I want to."

"Want to go?"

"Yes!" She jumped up. "Let me tell them we're leaving."

He chuckled and sighed with relief. He'd avoided a conversation with Claire's mother. Perhaps she subscribed to Claire's policy about letting the past stay in the past. Keep moving forward.

When they got to the Getty, it was crowded. As they hiked to the front of the museum, he took her hand. She had a little spring in her step and could have easily passed for someone in her early twenties.

Now that he'd found her again, he never, ever wanted to let her go again. He would have to take the job in Pittsburgh. It would be unprofessional to leave them without someone to fill in. But after that, he would have to find a way to get back to her.

Claire would not be single long. She was absolutely adorable. She was beautiful, smart, funny, and a great mother. He wondered if she wanted to have more children.

They reached the counter and he bought them two tickets to the museum.

Maybe it was her smile. Or her lithe figure. Or both. Whatever it was, Claire turned men's heads.

CLAIRE HAD SPENT countless hours here studying art.

She knew every crook and cranny of the public part of the museum. She even knew some of the private administrative parts, though it had been nearly twenty years since her days as a volunteer. She'd absorbed everything about the place.

She'd considered going to school to study art, but the more she learned, the less she thought it would be worth her time to invest in a degree. She had learned what she needed to know hands on.

She still wondered sometimes, if she'd made the right decision, especially when someone asked her where she studied. It was a question she rarely got now that she was successful. Perhaps the word had travelled.

She loved sharing her love of the museum with Grayson. She loved holding his hand as she navigated her way through the halls.

She also loved the way he looked at her. His attention never strayed. She could tell he scanned the crowds. Figured that was his military training. She would have expected no less. But his eyes stayed on her, especially when he wore that look of interest.

He'd always had that look for her. Since they were in high school.

Now that she was older, she knew how rare that was. That it was a gift. Very few people were fortunate to have someone who looked at them like that. Especially someone who looked like Grayson.

Tall, dark, and handsome.

She felt safe with him. No one was going to bother her while she was with him. Maine D'Court had come closest, but as soon as Grayson stepped up, he had stepped back. With her fingers looped in his, there was no question that they were together.

They stopped to admire a painting of two lovely ladies and he shifted to stand behind her, wrapping his arms around her.

She closed her eyes. Just for a minute. And enjoyed the feel of him against her.

"You can see the brushstrokes," he said.

Her eyes fluttered open and she focused on the painting. "It's beautiful," she said.

"I went to the Louvre when I was in Europe," he said.

She pulled away to look into his eyes. He released her. "I had no idea you liked art."

"I guess I had a little early influence," he said, sheepishly.

She thought back to their early days. Her eyes widened. "We did come here," she said. "I'd forgotten."

"On more than one occasion."

"If I recall, you weren't that into art."

"I was young. And getting ready to go into the military. I probably had some notion that it wasn't manly to like art."

She laughed. "I'm glad you saw the error of your ways."

"I actually like the architecture most of all. But I appreciate the art."

"I know what you mean. I'm drawn to the art, but I appreciate the sculptures for what they are. There's a difference."

They moved along to the next group of paintings. They spent the next two hours meandering through the museum, in no hurry. She could think of no place she'd rather be than there, at the museum, with Grayson.

It was nothing short of a small miracle that they have found each other again.

"Did you ever think we'd see each other again, much less get back together?"

"I wondered all the time. If I'd know you were divorced, I would have already looked for you."

"If you'd looked for me, you'd have known," she said, her lips bowed prettily.

"You're quite right."

"So how were you planning on finding out?"

"I'm a man. I didn't have a plan."

She laughed. "I thought you were happily married long ago and living with your wife and three kids."

"You remembered. I'm impressed."

"Why wouldn't I? I was planning to be that wife." She said the words before she thought. She bit her lip and fervently wished she could rewind and make the words go away.

"I was planning on you being that wife, too," he said.

She smiled, no longer thinking she'd said the wrong thing.

They walked a few feet. "So, we're back together?" he asked, a mischievous glint in his eyes.

She felt her cheeks heat with a blush. She had said that. "I just meant. Together. Like this."

"Do you want to be back together?" He asked.

"Do you?"

"I never wanted to be apart," he said.

"But you've had other girlfriends."

"You got married."

"Point well made. You never wanted to get married?"

"I toyed with the idea a few times, but no. I never dated anyone that I wanted to marry."

"Hmm."

"Hmm. What?"

"Nothing," she said. "I just thought you would have."

"Maybe I was waiting for you."

"Whatever," she said, moving away from him. "You weren't even looking for me."

"Waiting and looking don't have to be different things."

She leaned over a rail and wondered about the appeal of the painting in front of her. She often wondered about the appeal of paintings. Why some had mass market appeal and others didn't. It seemed to be whatever elicited emotion. Not about how well it was painted.

"The past is past," she said.

"Agreed."

"I'm hungry."

"Want some popcorn?"

AND JUST LIKE THAT, Grayson mused, they fell back in step. It had been surprisingly easy. Take the girl to a museum.

He laughed to himself. Not just any girl.

Claire.

Claire was the only girl he knew who would find going to the museum to be an entertaining afternoon. He knew girls that liked the casino. That liked to go shopping. He even knew a girl once who like to target practice.

But Claire was one of a kind.

In more ways than one.

She was the girl who always had his heart.

He got them popcorn from the concession stand and they walked outside through the gardens snacking on popcorn.

"Tell me about the Air Force," she said.

"That's something you don't want to know about."

"Why not?"

"Okay. I spent a lot of time jumping out of airplanes."

"Not just for the sake of jumping."

"At first it was. While we were training. Then after we were deployed, it was for rescue purposes."

"So, you also learned a lot about treating injuries, too."

"Yeah, that was a big part of it. And learning to treat injuries in less than ideal conditions."

"You liked it?"

"There's nothing else like it. The adrenalin is addictive."

"Do you want to go back?"

"No. It's for the younger guys. I'm too old now. I stopped after ten years and went back to school. Then I had to do another three years as an officer. But my days of jumping into danger ended a long time ago."

"Good."

"Good?"

"I don't like thinking about you being injured."

"The young guys don't even think about that part. We thought we were indestructible."

"I guess there are a few good things about getting older," she said.

They stopped and sat on a bench. Watched a butterfly flit about. Claire held out a hand and it landed on her fingertip.

"They say butterflies are a reminder to focus on the here and now," Grayson said.

Claire glanced at him out of the corner of her eye. "Then the butterfly is my mascot."

They sat quietly while the butterfly sat on Claire's fingertip. She shifted slightly, but it stayed. "I've never had this happen," she said. "Have you?"

"Never."

He leaned over and pressed his lips against hers.

She closed her eyes for the briefest of seconds. When she opened her eyes, the butterfly was gone.

"Here and now," she said, feeling the sadness in her eyes.

"Don't be sad," he said. "Our here and now is full of promise and happiness."

She smiled into his eyes. "Yes," she said. "Yes, it is."

They went back inside the museum, but decided they'd had enough for one day.

"Would you like to have dinner?" he asked. "I know a good little Italian place nearby."

"Yeah," she said. "That would be nice."

When he said *little Italian place*, he meant little. The place had red and white checkered table cloths, but the wait staff wore black tuxedos. It was an interesting combination of quaint and fancy.

After they ordered pasta, Claire brought up the obvious. "Do you have a place to live in Pittsburgh yet?"

"I have a couple of possibilities," he said.

"You went there for an interview?"

"I did. One of the professors is taking a year to go live and work in Japan, so he was the one who showed me around the city."

"I've never been there. Is it nice?"

"Surprisingly, yes. It's very pretty. After we left the university area, he took me downtown. We drove through a long tunnel. When we came out on the other side, the city was there, right in front of us. With the river right there below us."

"Don't they have more than one river?"

"There are three right there that come together."

"I never paid any attention to it. But it sounds intriguing."

"I thought so, too," he said.

"You must be excited."

"I was," he admitted. "But not so much now."

Their entrees arrived and they sat quietly enjoying their food for a few minutes.

"This is really good," she said.

"I'm glad you like it."

"Claire," he said. "If we can make it work for just one year, not even a year, just until next May, I can try to come back here. I can find something else."

She nodded, but kept her eyes down.

He kept talking. "I wouldn't go, but I don't have anything else here now and they're counting on me. The guy who's going to Japan said they hadn't had all that many applicants. Granted, that was March, but still, it sounds like they really need me to cover for him. He said if he can't find someone to cover for him, he can't go."

"Do you know why he wants to go?"

"I think he has a girlfriend there. He wants to bring her back here, but she can't leave yet. I didn't ask too many personal questions."

"I admire you for wanting to help him out," Claire said.

"I'm a sucker for a sad story, I guess."

She looked back up at him. "I guess so."

"We can do it, right? Am I missing something?"

"No. We can do it."

"You're hesitant."

"It just feels like déjà vu," she said.

"It does. Doesn't it? I'm so sorry for that. I'll so make it up to you."

"Okay," she said.

After dinner, he drove them back to her house and walked her to the door. They stood at the door for a moment.

"I'm going to just go inside," she said.

"Okay," he said, confusion on his face.

She tiptoed up to kiss him on the cheek. "Thank you for a lovely day," she said, then he turned and kissed her lightly on the lips. She went inside, leaving him standing there looking befuddled.

CLAIRE CLOSED the door behind her and leaned against it. She closed her eyes and pressed her fingertips to her lips.

It had been so easy to fall back into being a couple with Grayson. Too easy.

So easy it frightened her.

Then came the reminder. He was leaving. Again. Soon.

She locked the door and pushed away from it. She went into the living room and flopped down on the sofa.

People did long-distance relationships all the time. All. The. Time.

It wasn't like she didn't have the money to visit him. It wasn't about the money.

It was about all the evenings she would spend alone.

All the mornings she would wake up alone.

She'd spent nearly twenty years of her life in that kind of relationship.

It was not how she wanted to spend the next ten, twenty, or thirty years.

He said he could try to come back after a year. Try.

Once he was away, it became easier to stay away. He'd be lured by the next opportunity.

She knew. She'd been through it before.

It was different with Noah being a pilot, but there were too many similarities to what Grayson was proposing.

She couldn't ignore it.

Perhaps she should lay low for a bit. Play it cool. Stay away.

She scoffed.

She could no more stay away from Grayson Moore than a moth could stay away from a flame.

She could, however, disappear for a bit.

Pushing herself off the sofa, she went into her home office, turned on her computer, and sent the necessary emails and made the reservation

---

10

When they had gotten back to Claire's house, Grayson hadn't been sure how to proceed. He'd opened the car door for her and walked her to the door.

She'd meant to kiss him on the cheek, but he turned and caught the kiss on his lips. Their lips barely brushed against each other, but it was enough to leave him wanting more.

Then he waited while she went inside. After he heard the door lock click, he turned and went back down the sidewalk to his car.

He sat in his car, gripping the steering wheel and watched her door. She'd been quiet since they'd talked about his moving.

She'd brought it up. Something he hadn't been going to. He was going to focus on the moment.

He'd enjoyed spending the day with her. It had been easy to forget about their real world problems and just be together.

But now he was at a loss as to how to proceed.

Should he give her some space? Or should he go up and knock on her door?

It was gut-wrenching to think that they had less than two

months to spend together before he went away for a year. And here they were spending it apart.

Shoring up his resolve, he got out of the car and started up the sidewalk. A dog barked in the neighbor's yard and he jumped. Stopped.

Claire's downstair's light went off. He watched until the light upstairs come on. He couldn't see inside because she had closed the curtains, but the upstairs light was muted compared to the bright light downstairs.

He couldn't knock on the door now. It would be in poor taste to do so when she was getting ready for bed.

He sighed and turned around.

He would call her tomorrow.

THE NEXT MORNING, he sent her a text message. It was a simple *good morning* with a smiley face.

No response.

He dragged himself to his coffeepot and poured his second cup.

He had PowerPoint presentations to prepare.

He went back to his desk and sat down.

Maybe she was still asleep.

Danielle would be at orientation all day, so maybe Claire had turned her phone off.

He opened the textbook and began a new file on personality disorders.

Maybe she went out to work in her yard. Did Claire work in her yard?

Or did she hire her yard work done?

There were so many things he didn't know about her.

He googled images for borderline disorder. Copied a couple into the file.

Maybe she went for a jog.

Did she jog?

He checked his phone again. It showed her message was delivered.

He turned his phone over and went back to work. He managed to get through two personality disorders before he checked his phone again.

By the time he got through all ten, he'd talked himself into calling her. It was almost noon. Maybe she wanted to have lunch.

He dialed her number, but it went straight to voicemail.

He hung up.

Today was not going to be a good day.

If she was avoiding him, he needed to let her be.

Even with the possibility that something had happened to her, he couldn't very well just show up at her house. He'd promised he wouldn't do that. He could see already that was a promise he was going to have to break.

Too antsy to sit still, he gathered up his dirty clothes and turned on the washing machine. Then he changed his sheets.

And took out the garbage.

It had been all of twenty minutes.

Today was definitely not a good day.

He went to the kitchen to make a sandwich, but too late, realized he had nothing edible. Nothing but stale bread.

He pulled on a pair of jeans and a t-shirt, picked up his keys and drove to the supermarket.

It didn't take long to fill up his cart. He made sure he had plenty of food. Just in case someone stopped by.

After he checked out and loaded his car, he decided maybe he should drive by her house just make sure she was okay. He wouldn't stop. He'd respect her privacy.

He pulled up to the curb on the street in view of her house, but he had no way to tell if she was home or not. As always, her garage door was closed. Since it was daylight, he had no way of knowing if her lights were on.

Feeling a bit like a stalker, he drove away.

He drove home, put his groceries away, and decided he needed to clear his head.

He left his phone charging on his nightstand and, grabbing his keys, went out the door. The apartment complex was adjacent to a little woodsy park.

He walked among the trees a bit before finding a bench and sitting. No one else was out and about this afternoon. He supposed it was too warm for them, but after living in Texas, he enjoyed the weather.

Grayson needed to give Claire some space. She'd made that apparent. In his experience, a woman would ignore him for only one of two reasons. Either she wasn't into him or she hadn't decided yet. And really, he'd never experienced that second option, so he was tacking it onto his list to give Claire the benefit of the doubt.

He took a deep breath. He needed to be cool.

The ink was barely dry on her divorce papers. She'd been married and divorced. She'd had a child. And that child had been troubled recently. Those things would shift a person's perspective on life.

He'd been in the Air Force. He'd experienced traumatic experiences including watching people die. A lot of people. Good people. Men fighting for their country.

They weren't the same people as they had been in high school.

Besides, Claire ran in different social circles. She'd been married to a successful pilot and she'd established herself as a successful entrepreneur of not only an art gallery, but also a charity foundation.

He was a social worker teaching college kids.

Claire was a woman who made decisions with her head, not

her heart. Grayson wasn't a logical choice for her. The hormones that had connected them in high school may no longer be there or even more likely weren't strong enough for them as adults.

Especially since he was going away. Again.

Either way, he had to resign himself that she may not be invested in him this time around.

Some people couldn't, for whatever reason, reengage in a previous romance.

His resolve strengthened with a determination to let her contact him, he walked home.

He took his phone off the nightstand.

There was a message from Claire.

His heart skipped a beat.

I had to go out of town for a few days. I'll let you know when I get home.

He sent back a quick response. *Is everything okay?*

She responded immediately. *Yes. Don't worry.*

Don't worry. What was that supposed to mean?

He had about a thousand questions. Where was she? Was she alone? What was she doing? Why hadn't she mentioned that was planning to be out of town?

Remembering his resolve to play it cool, he stuck his phone in his back pocket. He went to his little home office desk and opened his computer. He heart sank when he saw that he had twenty-three emails from students.

He sat his phone on the desk and sat down to get to work. Before opening the first email, he sent a simple text to Claire. *Okay.*

Whatever it was she had to do, he had to leave her to it.

He had a presentation to prepare and emails to answer.

. . .

CLAIRE TOOK a taxi to the Metropolitan Museum of Art. She'd gotten caught in the early morning traffic of Manhattan. She didn't mind.

New York had such a different feel from L.A. New York had so much energy in such a small space.

She loved it.

She'd sometimes thought about renting a small apartment here, but the hotel was the more logical choice and had all the comforts without the headaches.

She paid the driver and stepped out in front of the museum. There was something about a museum that she found inexplicably heady.

Today was no different. It had been almost three years since she'd made the trip over to New York. She'd been trying to find the time to come back for quite some time.

After talking with Grayson and getting tangled up in her thoughts, she knew it was the perfect time for her to get away.

Danielle was stable and busy with school and a new boyfriend. The divorce was behind her. She could take a few days and immerse herself into art.

She had no meetings set up and no one in the art community knew she was here. She was dressed as a tourist and planned to spend the day merely meandering through the museum, going wherever her eyes led her.

After wandering for a couple of hours, she stopped and had lunch in the little café, then wandered some more. Before she even realized it, several more hours had passed and she needed to head back to the hotel.

Her mind was racing with ideas for her next show, so she barely noticed the traffic. She made a few notes on her phone.

She went back to her room and ordered a salad. Like L.A., there were plenty of vegan choices in New York.

While she waited for her dinner to arrive, she went to the balcony and stepped outside. The sun had set and Times

Square was lit up in all its glory. She was high enough that the sounds were slightly muted, but still distinctive.

This was something she would love to share with Grayson. The thought came out of nowhere and caught her off guard.

A sudden wave of loneliness swept over her. She'd been so engrossed in the museum all day, that she hadn't thought about him. At least not consciously.

But now that she was here, at the end the day, she missed him.

Room service brought her salad and panini along with a complimentary bottle of champagne. She almost refused the champagne, but instead set it next her on the little table while she ate. "Why not?" she said aloud. If Grayson was there, they probably would have gone out to dinner. But even if they'd decided to stay in, it would have been so much better to have him here.

She opened the champagne and poured the bubbly liquid into a glass watching the play of bubbles.

She checked her phone. Pulled up the text messages from Grayson. Other than to say *okay*, he hadn't texted since she'd told him not to worry.

Maybe jetting off to New York like that without telling him hadn't been the best idea. She'd just needed to get away. To think.

Her phone buzzed in her hand. It was Martie.

"Hello?"

"Sorry to bother you," Martie gushed. "But two new paintings just came in from a new artist."

"Are they any good?" she asked.

"They're stunning."

"Wow. Really? What's the artist's name?"

"Paul Bache."

"Thanks for telling me," she said.

"I just couldn't wait to tell you."

After they hung up the phone, Claire sipped the bubbly champagne.

Martie usually took new artists in stride. Maybe she was becoming more invested in the art world.

She picked up her phone and sent a quick text – *Send a picture.*

She took her wine glass and her phone and went to sit on the balcony.

A few minutes later, her phone buzzed again. She opened the text and a picture of Grayson popped up. He was on a balcony also, only it was dark behind him. Maybe a wooded area? She zoomed in, but couldn't tell. He had a sexy little sideways smile on his face.

Why would Martie send a picture of Grayson? Were they together?

She felt sick to her stomach. Had he gone to the studio looking for her and ended up going out with Martie?

Why had Martie sent her that picture instead of the painting?

Martie had seen him come into the studio to see her. Hadn't she?

She paced back inside and, scrolling through her messages, tried to make sense of the situation.

She stopped pacing. Oh. No! She had accidentally sent the picture request to Grayson.

She set the glass of champagne on the nightstand and climbed into the middle of the bed. This is why she never drank more than a sip or two. The last time she'd had a couple of drinks, Danielle had been... created.

She ran her hands over her face. Glanced at the bottle of champagne. She'd barely touched it.

She went to Martie's text thread and asked for a picture of the painting.

Martie said she'd send it tomorrow. She'd already left for

the day.

Claire sighed. What to do about Grayson.

He sent another text. *Do I get a picture of you?*

She gasped. Uh oh. She opened her camera app and held the camera out for a selfie. Should she smile or look serious? She tried a couple of poses and examined the pictures. Taking a deep breath, she sent him a picture.

He wrote back. *Where are you?*

New York

There was silence on the other end of the phone

Are you serious? He wrote back. *Why?*

Why indeed? *I needed to go to some museums.*

She laid back on the bed and waited.

I see. You didn't want to tell me?

No. She sent back.

Do you want me to come join you?

Claire giggled. Right. *You have to work tomorrow.*

So? He wrote. *So do you.*

Guess I won't be there.

Can I call?

She stared at the phone. No. She didn't need to talk to him right now.

I can't talk right now.

Are you alone?

She rolled onto her stomach. *Yes.*

Have you been drinking?

How could he possibly know that? *Why do you ask?*

You're being... funny.

I'm always funny.

Ha. Can I call? He asked again.

She didn't answer this time. She left her phone on the bed and went to the refrigerator for a bottle of water.

The phone rang while she was drinking water.

She stretched across the bed and picked up the phone.

"Hello."

"Well hi."

"Hi," he said. "So you're really in New York?"

"Sure."

"And you didn't want to tell me."

"I couldn't."

"Claire. You can tell me anything."

"Okay," she said.

"Right?"

"I was afraid."

His voice was serious. "I will never. Ever. Do anything to hurt you."

Her giddiness faded into tears. "It might be a little late," she said, her voice hoarse with unshed sobs.

"That was an accident. We were kids and didn't have any control over it. We aren't kids now. We're in control."

She inhaled deeply. Regained control of her emotions. "You're right," she said, her voice steady now.

"Claire, please don't run away from me again."

"I wasn't running away," she said, though she knew that was exactly what she had done.

"I want to be part of your life."

"You are part of my life."

"I want to be the part where you at least let me know when you're going to New York. Even if you don't invite to go with you. I understand that you sometimes need time alone."

She took a deep ragged breath. Did she dare let herself care about him again? Did she let him care about her? "Okay," she said.

He laughed. "Okay? What?"

"Okay. I'll tell you next time."

"Fair enough."

"Grayson? Are you sure you want to go down this route again?"

"I'm one hundred percent sure."

"Why?"

There was silence on the other end of the phone.

"I'll tell you when you get back."

"All right," Claire said.

"Please be careful over there."

"I will," she said.

"I'll talk to you tomorrow," he said and they hung up the line.

Claire sat on the hotel bed, holding her phone.

It had been such a long time since someone actually cared where she was and what she was doing. Sure, her daughter kept up with her, but that was different. Danielle didn't necessarily want to spend time with Claire, even though she wanted Claire to be there for her.

And Noah. Well, Noah had a tendency to do his own thing. She couldn't blame him, either, since that had been their agreement going in.

And despite the coldness of their marriage, Claire had never, not once, cheated. Although after their legal separation went into effect, they had both agreed that it was okay to date others, Claire hadn't been interested. She'd thrown herself into her work even more. And that was the time Danielle had needed her parents there for her. Claire had to give Noah points for dropping everything and being there every day for Danielle.

Claire found herself in an interesting spot. She had only been with two men in her life. She was divorced from one and the other wanted to resume their relationship after twenty years. Did people even do that?

It went against her keep moving forward policy.

Or did it?

Her thoughts were winding around themselves and she was getting tangled up in her own ideas.

She put on her pajamas and crawled under the blankets. She would have to think about this tomorrow.

Tomorrow was another day.

GRAYSON, too, got ready for bed, even though it was still early.

He looked at the picture she'd sent him and laughed to himself. She obviously had no idea there was an open bottle of champagne behind her. As far as he knew, Claire didn't drink alcohol. She'd played it cool by having a sip or two, but she never drank more. She was much too in control of herself.

The fact that he'd caught her drinking was an anomaly. Finding her in New York hadn't even occurred to him.

He'd been shocked when she asked him to send a picture.

He could only explain it by her use of alcohol.

He must have really gotten under her skin for her to run all the way across the country from him.

She didn't say anything about work or meetings. And she probably would have told him if she'd had a planned trip.

Now that he knew where she was and that she was safe, his resolve to let her have time to sort things out was even stronger. At least she was far away from the likes of that Maine D'Court artist.

Tomorrow was exam day. He had to get up early to make copies. He would have to think about setting up online testing next year. There was no reason not to update his classes. Giving tests online would be much more efficient.

Since everything was ready for tomorrow, he went online and bought three tickets to Saturday's Dodger's game. It was time to add a little excitement to their lives.

laire spent the next day at the Museum of Modern Arts. She got there in time for a seven thirty guided meditation session. She grabbed a mat and made herself comfortable in front of Claude Monet's *Water Lilies.* While relaxing her mind and clearing her thoughts, she wondered how something like this would go over at her studio. She'd put Martie on setting it up for a trial basis. It would get some people inside her studio who otherwise would probably never set foot inside. Maybe she could go a step further and host a yoga class. The more comfortable she could make people feel coming through her doors, the more clients she could culture.

This idea alone was worth the trip over.

That and having a conversation with Grayson that she probably never would have initiated face to face.

She blushed a little at the memory that she'd accidentally asked him to send her a picture. That was something she never would have done. She could only imagine what he must have thought.

After the meditation session, a man who looked vaguely familiar approached her.

"Claire Worthington?"

She didn't answer. She wasn't here in a business capacity. She was wearing jeans and canvas sneakers. No one was supposed to know she was here.

"I'm Allen Samuels. We met at a fundraiser here a few years ago."

"Right," she said. She recognized him as someone she'd met before. "You're with…"

"I'm with Dolls for Rags Foundation."

She remembered him then. Danielle had gotten a group in her high school involved in doing some fundraising for them. She'd spoken with Allen several times on the phone. He was about ten years older than she was and she'd always found him a pleasant man to work with. He wasn't bad to look at either.

"Of course," she said. "I remember you now. My mind was somewhere else."

"Understandably," he said. "I'm sorry to interrupt like this."

"I don't mind," she said.

"I've been meaning to call you about a collaborative project, so you can only imagine how surprised I was to see you here. It's almost like I conjured you up."

Claire laughed. "Perhaps you did."

"Do you want to get coffee?" he asked. "Or maybe lunch."

"Coffee sounds good, but I don't think anything is open yet," she said. In truth, she wanted to get the meeting with him over with so she could resume her wandering.

"I think they open for coffee for the meditation crowd."

They went to the Terrace and found a table next to the window with a clear view of the skyline and street below. Claire ordered a cappuccino while Allen ordered coffee.

"What did you have in mind?" she asked.

"Right the point, I see. Alright. I'm thinking of expanding Dolls for Rags out your way."

"Great. How can I help?"

He stretched out his legs and sipped his coffee. "I'm looking for a partner."

The hairs on the back of Claire's neck tingled. She'd never had the need for a partner. Never wanted to have a partner.

"You seem to be doing quite well on your own," she said.

"I am," he agreed. "But you see, my wife died recently and I'm just not enjoying the work like I used to."

"Oh," Claire said, burying her expression in her coffee cup.

"I know. It sounds like a sad story, so I won't bore you with it. But…" he waited until she looked up and met his gaze. "I heard through the grapevine that you're divorced now and I thought maybe we could become friends."

Claire bit her lip to keep from laughing out loud. It was the oddest proposal she had ever been presented with. Was he asking her to become a business partner or a romantic partner?

"I'm not sure what you're asking me," she said.

"Ah hell, I'm not either. But I've always been attracted to you. And we obviously share interests. I guess I was hoping we could work together or play a bit. Or both."

Claire laughed out loud. She couldn't help it. To his credit, he laughed with her.

Allen's… proposition was flattering. She'd known him for some time. He had a stellar reputation in the art community. She'd always found him attractive.

Now that his wife had passed away, he was doubtless considered an eligible bachelor.

Ideally, he was a perfect match for her. Same social standing. Same interests. Similar career goals. Age appropriate.

Yet, she couldn't stop thinking of a certain Air Force veteran with gorgeous blue eyes. He'd kissed her ever so lightly the night before she'd run away from him. He'd kissed her and awakened so many memories that intertwined with the unexpected longing for more. So many feelings that she had been overwhelmed.

"I'm flattered," she said, biting her lip to stop laughing. "But I'm here for a sort of personal pilgrimage."

"I understand," he said, holding his hands up. "No pressure." He picked up a little square napkin and wrote his name and phone number on it before sliding it toward her. He winked. "In case you change your mind."

He stood up and held out his hand. She placed her palm against his and he kissed the back of her hand.

She felt absolutely nothing, aside from a little discomfort. Her gaze darted around the room, but no one seemed to be paying them any heed.

"Until we meet again," he said.

"Take care of yourself, Allen," she said and meant it. He was a nice guy.

As he walked away, she folded the napkin and tucked it in her handbag. She turned her gaze back to the view as she finished her coffee.

Claire had been well-schooled in controlling strong emotions. She was quite good at keeping her feelings under control. Danielle had been the one exception to that for the most part.

The other exception had been Grayson. When they'd been together, she'd felt overwhelming love. Then, after she didn't hear from him, that emotion had turned to despair. She'd hidden it, of course. She'd hidden it so well, that she'd convinced herself that she was over him. And had ended up married to Noah.

She watched as a pigeon landed on a neighboring rooftop. Even here in the midst of the city, nature still ran its course.

She took a deep, ragged breath. It was natural to have feelings. Human.

Her parents had been wrong in sending her to etiquette classes. Well, perhaps they hadn't been wrong. There was certainly some merit in having control of strong emotions.

There was also merit in having feelings.

Claire had loved Grayson. She had never stopped loving him. Neither of them were to blame for what had happened to keep them apart all those years ago. Perhaps it had been divine intervention. They were who they were because of what happened. And because of Danielle, she wouldn't go back and change what had happened for anything.

The fact that they'd found each other again after twenty years was a major miracle in itself. They hadn't even been looking. It had been fate. It had to be.

Moving forward, she had no reason to deny herself what she felt for Grayson. In the great scheme of life, a few weeks with Grayson could be worth more than twenty years with someone else. If it led to a long-distance relationship, so what? She wasn't giving anything up.

Sure. She would be giving up the option of dating someone like Allen Samuels. But she didn't care about Allen Samuels. Or any of the other guys who might be out there.

There was only guy she cared about.

Grayson Moore.

And it was quality, not quantity.

She wanted to go home. Right now.

The streets of New York were alive with millions moving about.

She was in awe that there was only one person on this earth that she wanted to be with right now.

She closed her eyes as the emotions washed over her.

She was here. She may as well spend the day in the museum. She'd fly out in the morning.

She smiled at the way she instinctively went practical. Years of training and practice didn't disappear in an instant.

She sent a quick text to Grayson. *See you tomorrow?*

He wrote back in an instant. *Sounds perfect.*

She grinned. Thanks to modern technology, things were already different this time around.

WHEN CLAIRE ANSWERED the door the next evening, Grayson was in awe. Claire was wearing those yoga-type pants and a long t-shirt over them. She had on white canvas sneakers that she wore just about everywhere except to work. She had on no make-up and her hair was pulled back in a ponytail.

He'd never seen her look more beautiful.

It had to be the smile she wore. Unlike most of the time they'd spent together, she didn't have that air of suspiciousness about her. Her smile was all over her face. But mostly he noticed it in her eyes.

"You're beautiful," he said. She always was, but this was different. More relaxed. And open.

"I'm sorry," she said.

"Sorry for what?" he asked. What could she possibly have to be sorry about?

"I'm sorry I ran away."

He laughed. "I'm the one who should apologize. I'm the one who scared you away."

"I shouldn't be skittish," she said.

"It's cute."

"Come inside," she said and he followed her back to the kitchen. "I was just about to put something in the oven."

"Do you want some help?"

"Sure," she said, handing him her kitchen shears. "You can open this jar of artichokes and cut them into little pieces."

Grayson tested the lid. "I see why you wanted me over here. To open this jar."

She laughed. "Guilty."

"Do you have an old knife or screwdriver?"

He could open the jar, but didn't dare use what was no doubt expensive silverware in her collection.

She opened a drawer and pulled out a screwdriver. "Will this do?"

"Perfect." He rapped it in three places on the top of the lid and it popped open with a simple twist.

"I never can get that to work," she said.

"It's all in the wrist."

While he cut up artichokes, she buttered a deep casserole dish, added two packs of cherry tomatoes, and stirred in some crushed townhouse crackers. She added a few more pats of butter along with some sun-dried tomato vinaigrette salad dressing. "I never said it was exactly healthy," she said.

"Looks a lot healthier than how I usually eat," he admitted.

She added in spices and stirred in his artichokes, then put the whole thing in the oven.

"It looks good," he said. "What's it called?"

"I call it my sun-dried tomato dish," she said.

He took a step toward her and she didn't back away. He took another step and was now in her space. He tucked a strand of hair behind her ear and looked into those gorgeous green eyes. As he bent close, she closed her eyes and tilted her head up. He placed his lips next to the corner of her mouth. Her intake of breath was ragged. He put his arms around her and pulled her against him.

"Oh," he said. "I brought you something." He'd nearly forgotten.

"What is it?

He reached into his pocket and pulled out the tickets to the baseball game. "Tickets for Saturday's game," he said, fanning the three tickets.

"You got three," she said.

"Of course. You don't think I'd leave Danielle out, do you?"

She grinned. And wrapped her arms around him. "You're awesome."

Her phone rang. "It's Martie," she said.

"Go ahead," he said. "I'll just answer some student emails on my phone."

Claire wandered down the hall as she talked to her assistant. Grayson hadn't been exaggerating. He only thought he had a lot of emails to answer before the test. Turns out he was even more inundated after the test.

He couldn't understand why a student who hadn't had the time to prepare for an exam wanted to ask for more work. He politely stated that he had a policy against extra credit and let it go. While he typed, he sat down at Claire's breakfast table. After he finished answering all his emails, he set down his phone and waited.

His gaze wandered to a note pad where she had scribbled notes about yoga and meditation classes. Intrigued, he read over her notes. Her ideas were spot on.

Get people in. Get them comfortable.

And they become customers.

He heard her say the word *yoga* to Martie. Claire was one of the most driven people he had ever met. She didn't just talk about doing things. She did them.

He flipped the page, wondering what else she had come up with during her two days in New York museums. And there, tucked beneath the page was a napkin. A man's name and a phone number was scrawled across the napkin. The handwriting was definitely not Claire's.

Allen Samuels.

Hearing Claire wrapping up her conversation, he dropped the paper to conceal the napkin and picked up his phone. As she came in his direction, he stood up.

"That was Martie," she said. "We're starting up a meditation class."

"That sounds interesting," he said. Actually, it was fascinating, but he couldn't think past the buzzing in his ears. Had Claire picked up a guy while she was in New York?

While she checked the dish in the oven, she chatted about how she'd come up with the idea for the class. "I wish I'd thought of it myself," she said. "But I don't think there's anything wrong with building on an idea," she said, straightening to face him. Her face was alive with excitement.

"There's nothing wrong with it," he said. "I admire your grit in making things happen."

Some of the excitement faded from her expression as she watched him. He scrubbed at his face. "I need to borrow your restroom," he said.

He turned and strode to her restroom. He closed the door and stood there, inhaling deeply.

This was not good. He didn't want to be the guy who put a downer on his girl's ideas. Just the opposite. He was supportive. He loved her idea. He just couldn't get the thought of her meeting someone in New York out of his head.

Maybe he didn't really know her. He only knew who she used to be. Or what she appeared to be. He didn't know the circumstances of her divorce. He hadn't asked and didn't think it was his business.

Was Claire the kind of girl who went off and met guys on a whim?

His gut said no.

He splashed cool water on his face. In truth, they hadn't talked about their relationship being exclusive. Did adults even do that? In high school, they'd said they were "going together." When did they get to the point of not seeing other people? He'd just assumed they were exclusive.

Perhaps he had no right to do that. Perhaps it needed to be stated. Talked about. Considered.

It had been a couple of years since he'd had a steady

girlfriend. He couldn't even remember how they'd gotten to point of being steady. Or if they even had. He'd liked her, but he couldn't remember worrying too much about what she did with her own time.

Again, he had a tendency to make a lot of assumptions.

But not with Claire. He didn't want to mistakenly make assumptions. And he surely didn't want her going to New York or anywhere for that matter picking up men.

"Grayson, are you alright?" Claire asked from the other side of the door.

"I'm okay. I'll be out in a minute."

Whatever it was, he couldn't go all Neanderthal on her. He didn't know how she was coping with his leaving again.

He had to take it slow and let the relationship build. When the time was right, he'd bring it up and they could agree to be exclusive. Whatever people called it these days.

He would most definitely bring it up before he left for Pittsburgh.

Feeling much calmer now, he found her in the kitchen getting plates from the cabinet.

"Are you sure you're alright?" she asked. "You looked a little unwell for a minute."

"Yeah," he said. "I'm good. I'm probably just need to eat something."

"It's ready," she said.

"Great. Here," he said, reaching for the hot pad. "Let me get that out."

Some of the suspiciousness was back in her eyes. He kicked himself for that. She filled their plates with the tomato casserole and they went into the living room, and settled on the couch to eat.

"Wow. This is really, really good," he said, after the first bite.

She chucked. "You sound surprised."

"You're the one who self-professed not to do much cooking."

"Just because I don't do it much, doesn't mean I can't," she said with a mischievous smile.

"I'll have to remember that about you. You're a woman of many hidden talents."

"That's right," she said.

"Want to tell me about other hidden talents?" he asked. Even as he said the words, he knew he was headed down a path he'd told himself he wouldn't go.

"Oh no," she said, teasingly. "Discovery is the best part of the process."

"Is that so?" he asked.

"It is. Besides, think about how little I know about you," she said. "I haven't even been to your place. I don't have any idea how you live."

"It's nothing to get excited about," he said. "I promise."

"Maybe not, but you know everything about me. You know my decorating style. I don't even know what color hand towels you have."

"Hand towels?"

"Yeah. You know. Basic stuff."

He thought about his little apartment. And compared it to her fancy house. Once she saw how he lived, she may lose interest in him. He didn't and couldn't live the way she did. She had done a nice job of distracting him from the mysterious Allen Samuels. He may as well get it over with. His philosophy was to snap it off like a band-aid. If she didn't like that part of him, it was a good time to find out.

"Alright," he said. "Tomorrow then."

"Tomorrow then what?"

"Tomorrow I'll cook dinner for you at my house."

She looked at him sideways. "Okay," she said.

"Hey," he held up his hands. "It was your idea."

"So we're seeing each other three days in a row."

And he thought he was quick to cut to the chase. Seeing each other. That didn't sound quite as committed as going together.

He shrugged. "Unless you have something already planned." He sat back. "I shouldn't have assumed."

"No," she said. "I don't."

"We can wait. Take a break."

"No," she said. "I don't want to take a break."

"Claire," he said. "If you have something else going on, just tell me."

"I don't have anything else going on."

"If there's someone else in New York… it's okay."

She huffed out a breath. "There's not anyone in New York. I just needed to clear my head. That's all. I didn't even get out except to go to two museums."

He shouldn't ask about it directly. If he did, he'd be admitting that he'd looked through her papers. But… if he didn't ask about it, it was going to eat at him.

AFTER DINNER, Claire put their plates in the dishwasher. She couldn't figure out what was going on with Grayson.

He'd been different since she took the call from Martie. Was he jealous of work? He shouldn't be. He'd spent the time answering emails from students. Did he think Martie was someone else? Another man, perhaps?

"You know Martie's a girl, right?" She said suddenly, whirling around to face him.

"Of course," he said. "I met her, remember, at your fundraiser."

"Right," she said. Wiping off the cabinet. Still. Something was off. "That was Martie who called earlier."

"I know. You told me."

"Do you want to watch TV?" she asked.

"Sure."

They went into the living room and turned on the television. Whatever it was, it wasn't bad enough that he wanted to leave, but it was bad enough that he was acting distant.

"Was everything okay with your emails?" she asked.

"Yeah. Just normal questions from students."

"Then what's bothering you?"

He just stared at her.

"I'll get us some water," she said, standing up. She started toward the kitchen, then stopped and stood squarely in front of him. "I know something's bothering you. Since I talked to Martie. But I can't figure out what it could be."

"Something is bothering me, but I can't figure out how to tell you."

She crossed her arms. "That's better. Maybe you should just spit it out."

"I'm worried that you met someone in New York."

"Okay, maybe you should spit it out in such a way that it makes sense to me."

He inhaled deeply, locked his gaze on hers. "Alright. While you were talking to Martie I sat at your table and happened to see your notes about the yoga classes. I think it's an awesome idea, by the way. After I finished my emails, I was thinking about your classes and I read your notes." He paused. Waited.

"Okay," she said.

"I saw the phone number for Allen Samuels," he said.

"What phone...?" She must have left that napkin in her papers from her trip. He was worried about that? She snorted. Then bit her lip.

"What?"

"You should have just told me."

"I didn't want you to think I was snooping."

"I'd rather think you were snooping than acting all funny."

"Okay," he said.

"Allen gave me his phone number. He asked me to call him about a business deal. Then he started to hit on me. So I told him I wasn't interested."

"You kept the number."

"He's a business colleague whose wife recently passed away. I think he's going through some stuff."

"I see."

"Grayson, you have to tell me these things. You have to tell me what's bothering you and not keep it inside."

"You're right," he said.

"You teach this stuff, right?"

"I do. But helping others do it is a whole lot easier than doing it myself."

"Don't worry, okay?"

He stood up, pulled her close, and wrapped his arms around her. "Okay, my love, I won't worry. But I have an early meeting in the morning and I need to look over my notes for tomorrow's classes."

"You're leaving," she said against his shoulder.

He nudged her back a bit, and she saw the smile playing about his lips. "Don't worry, okay?"

"Ha. Point taken."

She walked him to the door. He kissed her goodnight. A gentle kiss on the lips. More. She wanted more. But he kissed her on the forehead and then he was gone. "Lock the door," he said as he stepped out.

She locked the door and set the alarm before she went back to sit on the couch and hugged a pillow to her.

It was early, but she should have heard from Danielle already. She sent her a text asking for her ETA.

Might sleep over at Joey's. Do you mind?

Yes. Instead she typed. *No. Just let me know.*

A couple of minutes later Danielle wrote back. *See you tomorrow.*

Another evening to herself. Her interactions with Grayson had felt off. That was the only way to describe it. The evening had started off well enough. Then after she'd talked to Martie, things had changed. He said it was because he'd found Allen Samuel's phone number. Surely he hadn't really been worried about that.

Then she remembered seeing a text come through on her ex-husband's phone. She still remembered the words. *Looking forward to our trip.*

He'd explained it away. It was a female pilot. Michelle maybe? Noah said they had a flight together – the first one in some time. He explained that Michelle tended to blur boundaries.

But more than the words and the explanation, she remembered the feeling. Just thinking about it brought that sick feeling back to the pit of her stomach. It was the kind of thing that never went away.

She got up, went into the kitchen, and found the napkin with Allen's phone number. She balled it up and tossed in the trash. She should have done that to start with. She'd thought they could work together. But Allen wasn't in a place to do that right now. Maybe later. If so, he could contact her. She wasn't hard to find.

There was nothing else she could do about it now. She just needed to give Grayson time. Time to believe her.

Keep moving forward.

12

*G*rayson drove straight home. He felt unsettled. He'd wanted his renewed relationship with Claire to be clean. That was the beauty of starting over. At least it should have been.

Instead he found himself worrying about things that probably didn't mean anything.

Probably.

The downside to starting over was the other side of the coin. He expected everything to slip into place without the normal getting to know each other stage. He was finding out that even with starting over, that phase couldn't be skipped.

It was going to take some time to blend their lives back together. That job in Pittsburgh loomed over his head. Like an angry deadline. He felt like they had to cram all the preliminary requirements to a long-term relationship into the few weeks before he left.

That was unrealistic. He needed to get his head straight.

The next morning after class, everything went off the tracks.

He had to stay through the afternoon to help out with

advising. It wasn't his day, but being the low man on the totem pole meant he had to take up the slack. Then the department chair called a meeting at the last minute.

It baffled him that the other faculty members didn't seem to mind the last minute request. One of the ladies even brought brownies.

The meeting did nothing but put Grayson in a foul mood. He had planned on getting home in time to clean his apartment before Claire came over. And he needed to go by the supermarket.

By five o'clock, they were still discussing the merits of changing their program requirements.

Grayson stepped out for a restroom break to send Claire a message. *Stuck in a meeting. Can we reschedule for another night?*

She responded quickly. *No problem.*

The timing on this was not good.

CLAIRE STEPPED out of her heels, sat down hard on the bed, and blew her bangs out of her eyes.

"Great," she said out loud. "Just great."

She'd left the museum early and stopped by the Blow Dry Bar. Her hair felt light, bouncy, and straight, with just a little flip on the ends.

She wanted to be mad, but she'd had it happen too many times before. How many times had Noah's flight been delayed? She couldn't even remember.

She unzipped her dress, but stopped when she caught a glimpse of herself in the mirror.

Another evening at home. Alone.

It seemed to be the way of things.

But the way of things didn't have to be.

She zipped her dress back up and put her shoes back on. Grabbing her handbag, she headed back downstairs.

She didn't have to go to New York. There was an exhibit tonight at the Natural History Museum that she'd been thinking about going to. If she left now, she could make it.

As she was backing out of her driveway, her phone buzzed. It was Martie asking her to stop by the gallery. *I need help with something. If you aren't busy.*

Claire sighed. Why did Martie always think she was available? Probably because she was. She wrote back, *I'll be right there.*

And why indeed was she always available? *I'm a business woman first,* she always told herself. The gallery was on the way to the museum. She could swing by, then head to the museum. She put her phone in her bag and set it on the seat beside her.

As she pulled onto the street, her phone buzzed again. "You'll just have to wait, Martie," she said out loud. "I'm on my way."

GRAYSON SAT IN THE MEETING, listening to the other faculty members go on and on about things no one could possibly really care about. He checked his watch.

He'd made a promise to Claire.

No faculty meeting was worth breaking a promise to the woman he loved. What kind of message would he be sending if he didn't show up tonight?

After the way things went last night, ditching out on her tonight was the worst possible thing he could do.

After five weeks, he would probably never even see these people again. Maybe at a conference. Maybe.

He fidgeted in his chair. Checked the time on his phone again.

He wouldn't do it.

He wouldn't cancel out on her like this. He didn't have time to clean his apartment or go to the supermarket, but that didn't mean they couldn't see each other.

He typed a message. *Since I didn't make it to the supermarket or have time to pick up my dirty socks, if I bring pizza, can I come over?*

He waited. Staring at his phone as though staring at it would cause her to respond. He waited five minutes. Ten. The faculty members droned on and on. Fifteen minutes and no response.

His decision made, he got up and quietly walked out of the meeting. As the door closed behind him, he heard them still talking, not a hitch in the conversation.

He got into his car and drove straight to Claire's house. He hated her garage. He couldn't tell if she was home or not. Since she hadn't answered his text, he decided not bring pizza.

He rang the doorbell. Waited.

Then he walked around to the backyard to see if there were any lights on. The house was dark. She definitely wasn't home. Unless she was asleep.

When she was home, the house was lit up like a baseball stadium.

Walking around aimlessly, he noticed there was a garage window. It was small, and over his head, but since he was in the backyard anyway, he decided to see if he could take a peek into the garage.

He had to drag a chair over from the patio and climb into it. He imagined the trouble he would be in if Claire came home and found him lying in her back yard, mangled from falling off a chair.

While peeking into her garage.

Of course, it could be days before she found him. He'd never known her to go outside much. She might notice him one day when she was taking out the trash.

At any rate, she wasn't home. The garage was empty.

Climbing down without mishap, he dragged the chair back to its rightful place.

He should go home. And try to call again tomorrow.

He wandered back around to the front of the house.

He would wait.

Since he was parked in her driveway, he realized she would know he was there. That was a relief. At least if he'd fallen in her backyard, she'd have known to go looking for him.

He went to the front steps of the house, sat down, and waited.

His stomach growled. Maybe he should have gotten the pizza after all. At least, then he would have something to eat. He thought about having something delivered, but somehow it seemed that would dilute the whole gesture of waiting for her.

He checked his phone. Answered some more emails. Did they never end? He sent one word answers – yes and no. At least they couldn't complain that he didn't answer in a timely manner, even on a Friday night.

He was reminded of one of his professors in graduate school, an older man nearing retirement who proclaimed email to be evil and the Internet to be the downfall of civilization. At the time he'd pitied the man. Now he understood completely. Unfortunately, the professor had been forced into retirement when he refused to teach online classes.

He reclined against the steps, his elbows propped behind him, his legs stretched out. He decided he should use the time to think about what he would say to Claire when she got home instead of worrying about old professors or student emails.

As the sun set and darkness settled over him, Grayson decided that grand gestures were sorely overrated.

He'd promised he wouldn't show up without calling first.

Perhaps he should try calling.

He quickly dismissed that idea and decided to stay the course. It would be much harder to ignore him if he was standing in front of her. Besides, there were exceptions to every promise.

BY THE TIME Claire had resolved Martie's dilemma, it was too late to make it to the museum.

Martie rarely had a dilemma she couldn't handle, but when one of the paintings had arrived with a rip in the top right-hand corner, she'd panicked.

"What do we do?" Martie asked, searching Claire's face.

"Did you call the artist?" Claire asked.

Martie's eyes widened with another wave of panic. "No way," she said.

"I'll call her," Claire decided.

When Claire got off the phone with the artist thirty minutes later, they'd decided to meet in the morning to assess whether the painting could be salvaged.

"Was she upset?" Martie asked.

"No, I mean, sure a little," Claire said, "but she understood that it wasn't anyone's fault. These things happen."

"It just had to happen to us."

Claire laughed. "Yes. It figures, doesn't it?"

It was getting late, so they locked up together, and Claire headed home.

When she pulled into her driveway, she had to slam on her brakes to keep from hitting the car parked in her driveway.

It looked like Grayson's car. Her heart did a little flip of anticipation, followed by a spurt of trepidation. Grayson said he was working late tonight. He wouldn't be here if he was working late.

The next thought was Danielle. She was supposed to be at her grandmother's house.

Claire dug her phone out of her bag and saw that she only

had the one message. The one she had thought was from Martie.

Which she now saw was from Grayson. Something about dirty socks and pizza.

She lifted her eyes from his message and saw him standing on her front porch.

How long had he been waiting?

She got out of her car and walked toward him. He slowly walked down the stairs, his hands in his pockets. As she got closer, she could see that he looked tired. And a little frustrated.

She would be frustrated, too, if she'd spent the evening waiting on someone's front porch.

They didn't say anything as they walked toward each other. Then his arms were around her, her face buried against his chest.

This. This was what she'd been searching for.

It was Grayson all along.

Not just today. Or last week.

But twenty years.

Since the night he'd kissed her and left her in her own bed to sneak down the hallway and out the back of her parent's house.

She remembered lying in the bed, her heart breaking. She'd cried that night. She'd cried like she'd never cried before while her body ached with new sensations.

After she'd finished crying, she'd focused on the promises he'd made. Promises to write. And call on the phone.

They'd be together again soon. He'd see her on leave.

That was the last time she'd heard from him for twenty years.

It hadn't been his fault. She knew that now. But even knowing it, the sting was still there.

Now with his arms around her, some of that sting was

beginning to heal. His touch soothed and comforted hurts that were buried so deep, they'd become part of her.

"I love you," he said against her ear.

She gripped him tighter, her hands fisting in his shirt and blinked back the tears, but she couldn't hold them back. The tears fell silently, dampening his shirt.

She didn't think it was possible, but he held her even more tightly against him.

Then he reached down and, putting an arm beneath her knees, picked her up and carried her up the front stairs of her house.

When they reached the door, he slid her to her feet. She reached out and touched the door knob to unlock it. He pushed it open and followed her inside. And waited while she locked the door from the inside.

Then he took her hand and led her to the sofa. He sat and pulled her into his lap. He kissed her forehead, her eyelids, then the corner of her mouth.

Then his lips were on hers and everything else faded away – yesterday and tomorrow. There was only right now. In this moment.

When they came up for air some time later, Grayson said, "I'm starving. Do you have anything to eat?"

Claire laughed. "I'm starving, too. Let's check the refrigerator."

Claire sat on a stool at her kitchen counter while Grayson grilled egg, cheese, and tomato sandwiches.

"It's a cross between an egg sandwich and a grilled cheese," he said.

"I think I have some potato chips," she said, going to the check the pantry.

"Not exactly vegan food," he said.

"As long as it's vegetarian, I'm good," she said.

He flipped the sandwiches over, then stepped over to kiss her on the nose. The gesture made her smile.

He was the only person who had ever kissed her on the nose. She remembered the first time. He was a football place kicker and she'd been a majorette. It was during a particularly close Friday night game.

She'd been standing on the sidelines in her little red uniform. The crowd was cheering as Grayson kicked and made the field goal, leading their team to a last minute victory. Grayson had walked across the field straight to where she was standing and in front of the crowd, cheering for his winning field goal, he'd kissed her right there on the tip of her nose.

The crowd had gone wild.

That kiss had been a famous moment at their high school. Someone had taken a picture and it had been displayed in the high school office. As far as she knew, it was still there. The tall football player and the petite majorette had a made a touching picture of high school sports and innocent young love.

"Do they still have the picture up?" Grayson asked as he pulled two plates from the cabinet.

Apparently, his thoughts had gone down the same path as hers.

"As far as I know."

"We were supposed to get married and have a house-full of kids," he said.

"I know," she said, "everyone thought it."

He took their plates to the table. As they sat next to each other, his eyes locked onto hers. "It's not too late," he said.

"What?" She laughed and took a bite of her sandwich.

"It's not too late."

"Really? You want to have a house full of kids? Now?"

"Well," he said. "Maybe not a house full. But I wouldn't mind having maybe one." He bit into a potato chip. "Or two. Or maybe three."

"Ha. Obviously, you've never been through childbirth."

"I never wanted children with anyone else."

She searched his eyes. Those beautiful blue eyes. And was speechless.

He shrugged and bit into his sandwich. "I'm just saying," he said a few seconds later.

"You're serious," she breathed.

"Eat. We'll talk about it later."

"Oh no. You can't say something like that, then just let it sit there," she said, but bit into her sandwich anyway. "Yum," she said. "This is really good."

He now had a smug look on his face. "I'm a really good cook," he said. "And as my sister can attest, I can change diapers, too. And I do so willingly."

"Are you auditioning?" she asked, amusement playing about her lips.

"Just watering some of those seeds," he said.

"What seeds?"

"Those seeds I planted back in the day. When I was a hot football star and you were a sexy little majorette."

She grinned. "You're still pretty hot."

"And you're still pretty sexy."

They finished eating and cleaned the kitchen together.

"What did you do with Danielle and Charlie?" he asked.

"Danielle is spending some time with her grandmother and she took Charlie with her. I may have to get another cat to keep me company when she's not here."

He dried his hands on the kitchen towel and pulled her to him. "I can keep you company."

She laughed as he kissed her ear.

"You are trouble, Grayson Moore."

"You like trouble."

"I must," she said.

"Then you're saying you like me," he said, kissing her face.

"Yes," she giggled. "I like you."

"That's good to know," he said, kissing her on the lips now. "I should go," he said.

"Uh huh," she said but he had her off balance and she couldn't think.

He took her hand and led her toward the door.

"Danielle is still going to the game with us tomorrow?"

"She wouldn't miss it for the world," she said.

"Good. I'll pick you up at five."

"Make it four so we can pick up Danielle," she said.

He kissed her again and walked out the door.

Before she could lock the door, he was back.

Her face broke into a smile as he kissed her.

"I have to move your car," he said. So much for romantic notions.

13

*G*rayson moved Claire's car aside, then backed his up to the road. He then pulled hers into the garage. After the garage door was safely closed, he used bringing her key around as an excuse to kiss her again.

He didn't want to leave. He wanted to stay and devour her.

But he knew it wasn't the way to do it. He'd professed his love and she'd remained silent. She was still coming around.

Grayson felt confident that she would. But first she had to reconcile their long-distance relationship. He knew better than to rush her.

He had no doubt that he wanted to marry her. He'd never had any doubt. He'd put the notion aside when she'd married Noah, but the minute he found out she was divorced, he'd known he had never stopped loving her and she was the only woman he ever wanted to marry.

There was just the minor problem of logistics. He had to go and she wouldn't go. Couldn't. She had too much invested here. A lifetime.

Grayson felt fortunate that he didn't feel ties to L.A. Hadn't felt ties, he corrected, until Claire walked back into his life.

He had to tamp down his sense of urgency to be with her and make up for lost time.

He stepped into his empty apartment and sighed. It wasn't much, but he had to live here a few more weeks. The next time Claire asked to spend time at his apartment, he would have no reason to hesitate.

He had too much energy to sleep, so he went into the kitchen, took out a box of black garbage bags and began the excavation process. He was moving soon, and unlike all the times he'd moved before, he wasn't going to take more than a few personal items other than clothes with him.

He started with the kitchen, throwing out old cans of food he was never going to eat and spices he'd had forever. From now on, he'd only be cooking with fresh food.

About midnight, he collapsed on the bed and napped a few hours before getting up early the next morning and resuming his house cleaning. He was a man on a mission.

He was ruthless in his closet as well. Everything except the necessities had to go. He must have hauled two dozen bags to the dumpster. The more he threw out, the more he wanted to throw out. It was most liberating.

Even his books. He chose six books he wanted to keep. The rest went in his car to take to campus to put on their give-away table.

He stopped when he came across an Apple iPad box in the back of his closet. The box itself had changed over the years, but the contents had not.

He sat on the edge of his bed and opened it up. There was copy of the picture when he had kissed Claire on the nose at the high school football game. He didn't even know if Claire had been given a copy. His coach had given him this one. There was their photo from senior prom. He looked a little goofy in his burgundy tux, but she had been lovely in her pink dress.

He'd kept every note she'd written him in high school. It

was from the days before text messages, so he had a stack of scraps torn from her notebooks. One simply said. "hi."

There was one, though, that had been written on blue paper. He carefully unfolded it and read the words she had written so very long ago:

Dear Grayson,

I wish you didn't have to leave, but I know you have to. You have to do your duty for our country. When you get back, I'll be here. I only ask that you stay in touch with me. Let me know what you're doing. What you're thinking.

And I need to know that you're safe.

I love you with all my heart. I always will.

He refolded the letter into its well-worn grooves. This letter had gotten him past countless battle wounds. Wounds that weren't visible to anyone who looked from the outside. The only way to see these wounds was to dip deep into his psyche. Knowing that Claire was there waiting for him even though she never wrote back had been enough to keep him going.

He only had to do four years and he would be out.

He'd gotten the letter from his mother with the newspaper clipping tucked inside only two days before he had to sign his discharge papers.

By the time he went into the office to meet with his superior, he'd made up his mind. He now had no reason to get out of the Air Force. He could make a good career in the military.

After that, he couldn't bear to look at the letter, but he couldn't bear to get rid of it either. So, he'd tucked it away in the shoe box he carried around with him.

After the shoe box started falling apart, he stuffed it all in a sturdy Apple box.

But it had been a really long time since he'd taken the time to pull the notes and letters out and read them.

She'd asked him to stay in touch with her. Nothing more. Nothing less.

And despite his best efforts, he'd failed to do just that.

This time when he was gone for a year – not four years – he would make sure he stayed in touch. He would call her every day and he would text throughout the day. He'd tell her what he was doing. In fact, he would start that habit right now.

Hi. He texted. *How is your day going?*

Running errands. She wrote back.

He smiled. This was going well already. *I've been cleaning my apartment.*

Ugh. I would not want to trade.

Still ready at 4:00?

Yes. Time for me to head home. She wrote.

He sent back a smiley face emoji and went to get into the shower.

CLAIRE PUT up her groceries and got into the shower. She hummed to herself as she washed her hair. Nothing in particular, just a catchy little tune she'd heard on the radio while she was out doing errands.

She'd been pleasantly surprised to hear from Grayson in the middle of the day.

Perhaps this thing with them had possibilities.

After her shower, she put on a pair of jeans, a T-shirt, and layered with a light sweater. She put on her favorite white canvas sneakers.

Just as she finished her make-up and put on her earrings, the doorbell rang. Grayson was right on time.

As he drove to her mother's house, he told her about how he'd gone through his apartment and purged everything he didn't need.

"I did that before I moved into my current house. I can't stand to live in clutter."

"It's a good thing I got it done before you came over," he said, a horrified look on his face.

She laughed. "I don't judge. Have you seen Danielle's room?"

"Actually, yes," he laughed.

They didn't talk about the fact that he would be leaving soon or that his real motivation was probably getting ready to pack up his apartment.

Claire thought maybe if they didn't talk about it, it wouldn't be what their relationship centered around.

They pulled into her mother's circle drive. "This is a huge house for one person," he commented.

"I know. I wonder if she keeps it for Danielle. Danielle loves the swimming pool."

"I bet she does," he said.

GRAYSON TRIED to ignore the trepidation he felt at driving up to Mrs. Beauchamp's house. It was the same house Claire had grown up in.

And he was still a little afraid of Claire's mother.

When they went inside, Claire went upstairs to help Danielle with something.

Grayson was left to follow Betty to the kitchen.

"How are you, Grayson?" Betty asked.

"I'm good." He was a soldier. He sucked up his fear and surged forward.

"Danielle tells me you're going to be moving across the country soon."

"Unfortunately, yes."

"Sounds a little familiar," she said.

Grayson winced. This was why he was afraid of Betty.

"I'm only going to be gone for a year," he said.

Would you like something to drink?" she asked.

"Water would be great, thank you," he said.

She handed him a bottle of water. "Grayson," she said. "I apologize for what I did. I overstepped my boundaries when I hid your letters and calls from Claire."

"It was a long time ago," he said as they sat at the kitchen table.

"Nonetheless, I wouldn't blame you if you never forgave me."

"I forgive you, Mrs. Beauchamp. It changed the direction of our lives, but Claire and I are who we are now because of it. And Claire has Danielle. Even I wouldn't change that."

"You're a kind man," she said. "I'll always regret the way I wronged you and Claire, Danielle notwithstanding."

"It means a lot for you to say that," he said.

"If it matters, I'm fully supportive of you now. I know how much Claire cares for you and I'll do everything I can to make up the wrong I did to you both."

"Mrs. Beauchamp."

"Please call me Betty," she said, putting a hand over his.

"Betty," he said. "Claire and I are working this out between us and I want you to know, from the bottom of my heart, that I forgive you."

"You're a good man, Grayson Moore. I truly hope that you and Claire can make a go of it this time."

CLAIRE STOPPED at the kitchen door when she heard their voices. Their conversation brought tears to her eyes.

She blinked back the tears and took a deep steadying breath. With a smile on her face, she walked into the kitchen. "What are you two up to?"

"Just catching up," her mother said.

"You look so serious. And here we are getting ready to go to my very first baseball game."

"You're kidding?" Grayson asked.

"Nope," she said. "I've never been."

"I'm glad you told me," he said. "I'll make sure you have the whole experience."

"I'll get Danielle so we can get going," she said. *And give them time to finish up their conversation.*

THEY ATE peanuts and Claire even sipped a beer. Danielle and Grayson ate hot dogs. This was after they had eaten Mexican food at the restaurant on their way to the stadium.

There was so much energy at the game. Claire hadn't expected that. On television, the game always seemed to move so slowly. She'd never actually been to a live baseball game. That had been Danielle and Noah's thing.

Grayson had gotten them really good seats. They were close enough – in the lower level directly behind the dugout - to actually see what was going on.

Danielle obviously enjoyed it. She'd even put her phone in her jacket pocket. Danielle and Grayson talked lingo while Claire listened, watched the game, and watched the crowd.

And reflected. She was glad that Grayson and her mother had talked. She felt like things were smoothed over with them now. Her mother seemed to accept that Grayson was back in her life and she didn't seem to have a problem with it.

On the contrary, she seemed rather contrite about what she had done and she appeared to welcome Grayson back.

It was one less thing preventing Claire from completely forgiving him and moving forward with their relationship.

"Mom look!" Danielle said, pointing to the screen.

As Claire looked, the image zoomed in and she was looking at herself and Grayson. Grayson was watching the screen, too.

In the next instant, there was a heart drawn around them the word kiss over their heads.

Grayson turned and putting one hand behind her head pulled her to him and kissed her nose. Then he pressed his lips against hers and pulled her close into a kiss that could in no way be G-rated. The crowd cheered.

He pulled back and smiled into her eyes. Over the pounding in her ears, she heard him say those words again. "I love you."

And this time, she said them back.

14

The next few weeks went by in a blur. Claire and Grayson became attached at the hip when they weren't working. When they were at work, they texted throughout the day.

They quickly got into a rhythm. Work during the week, evenings spent at her house, mostly, though sometimes at his. They cooked together, watched movies, and TV, and sometimes they just sat quietly and read, cuddled up together on the sofa.

On the weekends, they got out, had dinner, went to museums, plays, even an airshow. Sometimes Danielle went with them and sometimes they went alone.

Either way, they forged their way as a couple.

Claire stood at her bathroom counter running a flat iron through her hair. They had two weeks left together. She tried not to think about it, but she couldn't stop herself. It was almost like being on a mental countdown.

She hated it.

She didn't, however, tell Grayson.

Grayson showed up a little after five o'clock. When she opened the door, he handed her a red rose.

"It's beautiful," she said, taking it from him. Smiling, she took it to the kitchen and slipped it into the vase along with the one he'd brought her yesterday. She slid the vase back to the center of the kitchen table.

Then she was in his arms.

"I was thinking," he said.

"Uh oh."

"What? You like most of my ideas," he said.

She laughed against his chest.

"Okay," he said, "running in the marathon wasn't my best idea."

"Hey, I did the best I could."

"You might like this idea better. It's something I've always wanted to do."

"Tell me," she said, under the pretense of being skeptical. In truth, she'd been impressed with his creativity at finding things for them to do.

"This weekend," he said, nuzzling her neck.

"Yes?"

"We could rent a car and drive up to San Francisco – along the coast. And we could fly back."

This was unexpected. They hadn't left the area. In fact, they hadn't even spent the night together. "And what would we do in San Francisco?"

"We could ride bicycles across the Golden Gate Bridge and spend the weekend at Sausalito."

A weekend with Grayson in Sausalito. Alone. A whole weekend. "Okay," she said.

"Really?" he took her hands in his and grinned.

His smile was contagious. "Sure. Why not? It sounds like fun."

"So… can you leave in the morning?"

She almost automatically said no. But there was nothing going on at the gallery this weekend. Nothing going on tomorrow. Martie could handle the routine. Danielle was busy doing her own thing. "Yeah," she said, surprising herself. "I think I can."

"Cool," he said. "I'll make reservations."

While Claire boiled water for pasta and washed salad greens, Grayson sat at the table and, using his iPad, made reservations to rent a car and flight reservations to get them back on Sunday.

"I think the drive down will be nice," he said, "but I'd rather spend the morning on the island than driving back."

"I agree. It's a good idea."

There were four hotels in Sausalito. He picked the Cavallo Point Hotel. This one looks like it has the best view," he said, holding the iPad so she could watch the video.

"It looks really nice," she said. "I've only been to San Francisco a couple of times, but I always flew and I never got to the bridge."

"I've been once, but it was a quick drive and I always wanted to get back and bicycle over."

Biting her lip, she drained the pasta. This was Grayson's last weekend before he left for Pittsburgh. He had been crossing items off his bucket list for the last few weeks. There was no way he could maintain this level of activity week after week. Going to Sausalito was a big one.

He'd said he would be coming back here after the year was up, but something told her he didn't really believe it.

"It'll be fun," she said. "As long we can take breaks. I haven't ridden a bicycle since I was a kid."

He hugged her. "We can go as slow as you want to. I just want to spend time with you and make you happy."

She wanted to tell him that they could stay right where they were and she would be perfectly content. But he seemed to have his heart set on making the trip. She lifted her face to kiss him. "It'll be fun."

"Let's see if I can get a reservation," he said.

While he was online, his phone buzzed. He let it go to voicemail.

"Do you need to answer that?" she asked.

"Nah. It's probably a student." But when it buzzed a second time indicating voicemail, he picked it up and checked it. "Students usually text..." he said. Then grew quiet as he listened to the message.

"What is it?" she asked when he put his phone down.

He shook his head. "Odd. I just got another job offer."

"What? How? I didn't know you'd had any other interviews."

"In San Antonio. I interviewed with them back in April."

"You should call them back."

He picked up his phone and paced toward the living room. She could hear him talking as he paced.

He hung up the phone and came back to the table and opened his iPad.

"Well?" she said.

"The person they had hired had to pull out at the last minute, so, since I was their second choice, they called me."

"You told them you had a job, right?"

"Right."

San Antonio wasn't significantly closer than Pittsburgh. Anything outside of L.A. and it didn't matter.

Five minutes later, he had a room reserved. "I think this room has a good view," he said. "I'm surprised they had anything available."

"Me too," she said.

After dinner, they snuggled a few minutes on the sofa, but they were both eager to start packing. Claire had to call Martie and Danielle to let them know she would be out for the weekend. This was different from her *business trip* to New York. In fact, she couldn't remember the last time she'd been away for a weekend for fun.

As she talked on the phone getting everything set up, she stared at her clothes trying to decide what to take.

After she hung up the phone, she quickly filled up her suitcase with everything from jeans to a sundress to casual pants. When she got to her pajama drawer, decisions became a little trickier. She usually slept in shorts and T-shirt. She wasn't out to seduce Grayson and even if she was, she didn't own anything that would fall into that category.

She had a pair of cotton pajamas she'd only worn once. They were conservative enough that she would feel comfortable in them. And not feel like she was trying to be seductive.

Not that she would mind. They had somehow made a tacit agreement not to go too far. The other time, they had been kids with raging hormones and delusions that marriage would follow.

Now, they were complicated adults. Even with tentative plans to stay together, both of them knew, at least Claire knew, that everything was uncertain right now. It was best if they didn't complicate things with sex.

Having done everything she could do tonight, she decided it would be best if she was well rested. She could finish packing in the morning.

Although she'd been a little reluctant about the trip, she woke early the next morning with a sense of excited anticipation. A whole weekend alone with Grayson.

The very idea quickened her pulse. The fact that it was their last weekend together before he left next week made this trip seem all the more bittersweet.

He pulled into the driveway at eight o'clock in a rented

SUV. When she opened the door, he swung her around in a hug that swept her off her feet.

It was like they were two kids getting away for the weekend.

He took her suitcases to the car while she locked up. Danielle had Charlie at her grandmother's again, so there was nothing to worry about.

They chatted about everything and nothing as they headed north out of town. He took Highway 101 – the scenic route. It would take a little longer to get there, but Claire deemed the view of the coast well worth the extra time.

It was late afternoon when they checked into the hotel. Grayson had been right. They had an awesome view of the bay.

The room had only one bed – a king bed. Something neither of them said anything about.

"What are we doing first?" Claire asked, as she unpacked her suitcase, wondering if she should change.

"I thought we'd just walk around, get something to eat," he said.

"I should be able to wear this?" She ran a hand along her jeans.

"Sure. Looks perfect."

She added a light short cardigan, and after freshening up, came back to stand next to him at the window.

"Are you okay?" she asked.

"I'm great," he said, pulling her against him.

"It was a beautiful drive and I'm glad we did it," she said. "but I have to admit I'm glad we're flying back Sunday."

"I agree," he said. "It's always fun to start out on a trip, but going home can sometimes be something of a downer."

Claire laughed. "I know what you mean."

"Ready?" he asked.

They drove downtown and parked. Claire had never been to Sausalito. It was a quaint little town with some tourist shops and restaurants and lots of tourists walking about. They found a restaurant on the water. It had white table clothes and servers all in black. Grayson had been relatively quiet since they'd gotten to the room.

GRAYSON KNEW they needed to talk. He knew he'd been putting it off for several weeks, but time was running short.

"Can I order you a drink?" he asked, when the server stopped at their table.

She hesitated a moment. "Sure. I'll have a cosmopolitan."

Grayson order a martini. "We'll have to ride the ferry back after we bike over to San Fran."

"I hear the ferry is nice," she said. "Nice views of the bridge."

The server brought their drinks. Grayson held his up in a toast. "To us," he said.

They clinked glasses and Claire sipped her pretty pink drink.

"Something's bothering you," she said.

"Yeah," he agreed. "And if it isn't bothering you, we've got a problem."

She set her drink down. Sat up a little straighter. "You're leaving next week."

He nodded. "I'm thinking we should talk about it."

"We should," she said.

But they didn't. They sipped their drinks. Grayson was glad he'd ordered a drink. He'd been dreading this conversation.

"You might as well spit it out," Claire said.

He chuckled. "I guess there isn't much to say."

Claire rolled her eyes. "Grayson Moore you're not going to get away with that line."

He laughed. "You're right. So... I've got some money saved to fly over at least once a month."

Claire put her hand over his. "Grayson no."

"You don't want me to visit?"

"Of course, I do. I just didn't think about…. I don't want you to spend your savings on the flights. I could buy…"

He cut her off. "No. Don't even think it. I won't come if I can't pay my own way."

"Okay," she said, sitting back. "Then I can come there."

"That's kind of the same thing. I can't let you spend your money coming to see me."

"Then I guess we'll be talking on the phone a lot."

CLAIRE SWALLOWED the lump in her throat. If Grayson was going to be difficult, then this move wasn't going to go as smoothly as she had hoped. "Why don't we think about it and talk about it on the way home? I don't want to ruin our trip."

He finished off his drink and nodded.

"I'd like to walk around and get Danielle a T-shirt," Claire said, to lighten the mood.

"Sure," he said, but his smile was tight.

Claire had been through enough counseling with her ex-husband and her daughter to figure out that tension was running high between them right now because neither of them wanted to admit that they probably would see each other only occasionally after this weekend.

She'd been putting off allowing herself to think about it, but that was no longer an option.

We have this weekend, she told herself. The best thing they could do was to make the most of it. Focus on the here and now.

During dinner she chatted about the museum and how well the meditation and yoga classes were going. She chatted about the next fundraiser coming up in September. And tried to ignore the unpleasant thought than Grayson most likely wouldn't be there for it.

As she talked, she braced herself for this being their last weekend together. Period.

If he was worried about money, she wouldn't let him come visit and she wouldn't visit him. At the end of the academic year, they would see where they were.

If he came back to L.A., he came back. If he didn't then she couldn't hold it against him. He had a career. A career that was in a lot of ways she'd never considered, was a lot like the military. He could request a certain location, but he had to be prepared to go wherever the next job was. He might very well end up in Georgia or Maine. There was no guarantee there would be anything open in L.A. The fact that he'd taken a one-year temporary two years in a row wasn't a good sign.

She couldn't very well ask him to do anything different. That would be like asking her to do something besides her gallery. It was in her blood. She had no choice.

After dinner, they walked downtown hand-in-hand and wandered through the shops. She kept her negative thoughts to herself. As a result, they had very little conversation. She bought Danielle a T-shirt that smelled like coffee – on purpose. The coffee beans were baked into the material.

It didn't take long to go through the shops, so they drove back to the hotel.

Claire disappeared into the bathroom to wash up and put on her pajamas.

When she came back out, Grayson was sitting in a chair patiently waiting for her.

"Come here," he said, patting his knee.

He squeezed her against him. She wrapped her arms around him and held on.

He picked her up and carried her to the bed, tucking her beneath the covers. Then he went around to the other side of the bed and climbed in. He lay there for a minute staring at the ceiling.

Then he shifted over, took her in his arms again, and put his lips on hers.

They fell asleep kissing.

When Claire woke the next morning, her first response was panic. She was wrapped in a vise-grip. When she realized she was wrapped in Grayson's arms, she relaxed.

The morning sun was peeking through the gap in the curtains. She had no idea how late they'd stayed up kissing. But her lips were swollen.

One thing hadn't changed. She couldn't get enough of kissing him.

She maneuvered her way out of his arms and went to get into the shower. Today was going to be a challenge for Claire. Her idea of exercise was yoga. On a mat. In an air-conditioned room.

She'd ridden a bicycle as a kid, but truly, it had never been her thing. She'd quickly gotten bored with riding around the block.

Fortunately, riding across the Golden Gate Bridge was a far cry from riding around the neighborhood. And anything she did with Grayson was good. Well, running the marathon had been the exception to that rule.

After they got dressed, they went downstairs for coffee and breakfast. Grayson seemed less tense today. Some of his excitement was back.

When they got to the bicycle rental shop, she was the one who was a bit nervous and he was ready to get going.

The man at the shop gave her a rubber band. "What is this for?" she asked.

"It's to tie your pants to your leg so they won't get caught in the spokes," Grayson said.

Oh boy. There was so much she didn't know.

When they got on their bikes, she was a little wobbly.

"I don't know about this," she said as they rolled out of the parking lot.

He laughed. "Come on, Claire, you can do it. Let's get to the trail, then we'll stop and rest."

As they rode a few minutes, she became a little steadier, but didn't care for riding along the traffic. The cars rushing by made her nervous. She didn't know when she would fall. She couldn't help imagining hitting a rock and tumbling over – right in front of a car.

"Grayson," she said. "Don't they have a trail or something?"

"It's up ahead. Don't worry. They're used to cyclists. They won't run over you."

"I'm glad you're so confident," she muttered under her breath and heard him laughing.

Fortunately, they made it off the streets and to the trail without mishap. Going uphill, however, proved to be quite strenuous.

Before they got on the bridge, they stopped and rested.

"You can tell I've never done anything like this before," she said, taking out her water bottle. "Somehow I pictured us just hopping up on the bridge and riding across. I didn't think about having to get all the way to the bridge."

"I didn't do a very good job of preparing you." he commented. "But," he said. "I brought trail mix." He pulled out a package of nuts and dried fruit from his back pack.

"I wondered what you had in there," Claire said.

"Always prepared," he said. "I have a first aid kit, too," he said with a wink.

She rolled her eyes. "I thought you were confident about this thing."

"I am confident, but, you know, things happen."

"It's a beautiful day," she said. The sky was clear blue and the weather couldn't have been more perfect for an outdoor activity. The trail to the bridge was crowded with other cyclists as well as people walking.

When they rode onto the bridge and the bay unfolded below them, she caught her breath. "Wow," she said, steering to the side of the trail and stopping. Grayson, following her, rolled up beside her and stopped.

"Yeah."

The skyline of San Francisco was in the distance, but it was the bay below that was truly magnificent.

They began their ride on the bridge and the wind whipped up. Claire wondered if it was going to topple her over.

"Are you okay?" Grayson asked, coming up alongside her.

"Yes," she said.

As they went around the first pylon, the wind was so strong she had to get off her bicycle and push it. She stopped to gaze below at the churning water below. "Wow," she said.

He came close enough to kiss her. "I'm glad you're with me," he said. "What do you think?"

She smiled. And squeezed his hand. "It's so much higher than I expected. I love it."

"Did you notice?" he said, indicating the water below. "They added netting so no one can jump."

"That was a good idea. I wonder if they've had to use it."

"I'm sure they have."

When they got to the other side of the bridge, Claire was exhausted. Her legs ached. They stopped for a few minutes to admire the view back toward Sausalito.

But... it turns out they had a long way left to go. They had to ride to Fisherman's Wharf to catch the ferry back.

Four hours later from the time they'd rented their bikes, they made it to Fisherman's Wharf. They found a place to leave their bikes so they could walk around a bit and get lunch.

They stopped at a busy café on the wharf and settled in for lunch.

"So, I was thinking," Grayson said. "Since it's such a pretty day, we should ride our bikes back across the bridge."

She made a face. "You go ahead. I'm taking the ferry."

He laughed.

"I think that was one of the most awesome things I've ever done," she said.

"Truly?"

"Truly."

The server came and Claire ordered a soda. After she left, Grayson said, "I think I'm going to fall out of my chair."

"What?" she asked, innocently.

"Claire Worthington ordered a soda."

"A monumental achievement calls for a celebration."

"How long has it been?" he asked.

She shrugged. "I don't know. Fifteen years. Twenty. Maybe more."

"It's got to be more. Because I've never known you to drink a soda."

She laughed. "I guess I can still surprise you."

"You surprise me every day," he said, taking her hand and kissing her knuckles. "I'm so going to miss you," he said.

His words sent a stab into her heart. They'd gotten close these past few weeks. They'd seen each other every day.

"Hey," he said, seeing her expression. "We'll still see each other."

"Not every day," she said.

"No, not every day."

Her heart ached. "It won't be the same," she said.

"I think I finally discovered the secret to getting you to open up to me," he said.

"What's that?"

"Get you so exhausted you can't control your emotions."

"You might be right," she said. "Exhausted and hungry."

They ordered sandwiches and Claire sipped her soda

through a straw. "I'd forgotten how good a coke could be," she said.

"It's good to live a little, isn't it?" he said.

She had a feeling she knew where his mind was going. They'd been here before.

"No," she said.

"No, what?" He asked picking up a French fry.

"Whatever it was you were thinking."

"I was thinking that when we get back to Sausalito, we should have ice cream."

"Right," she said.

They ate in silence a few minutes.

"So, really, what do you think I'm thinking?" He asked.

"I think you're thinking that since you're leaving, we should live a little. You know."

"We are living a little."

She decided to let it go. Maybe she was imagining things.

"I think you're the one with dirty thoughts," he said.

She nearly spit out her coke. "Ah ha," she said. "Your mind did go there."

"Yours went there first."

"Is that so?"

"In the last hour, yes. It's true. But overall, probably not so much."

She laughed. "I'm gonna miss you, too."

"I hope so," he said. "But I'm planning on…" He stopped and gazed out the window of the café.

"Planning on what?" she asked.

He turned back and gazed into her eyes. "I don't know how to ask you this."

She set down her glass, overcome with trepidation. He looked so serious.

"What is it?"

He squeezed her hand. "I don't know what it's called anymore."

She frowned. "Give me a hint."

"We called it going together."

"You're talking about an exclusive relationship?"

"Yes," he said. "that."

Relief washed over her, followed by worry. She wasn't sure if he wanted to see each other exclusively or if he wanted to see others. She went with the latter. "You want to see other people."

"What? No! I don't even want to talk to anybody but you."

Relief. It washed over her like a balm.

"So…" he said. "Will you be my girl?"

"I thought I was your girl," she said, a smile playing at her lips.

He kissed her – a brief peck on the lips, but his face lit up. "So, that means we can make last minute plans and not have to worry about it."

"Grayson," she said. "You've had that since the day Danielle reintroduced us."

THEY GOT their bicycles on the ferry along with about one hundred other people and made their way to the top level to find a seat. Claire was physically exhausted.

The Golden Gate Bridge was to their left. It was majestic and Claire as in awe that just that morning that had ridden bicycles across it. The fog was coming in now and the bridge was partly obstructed by it.

Grayson nudged her. "See there," he pointed toward the bridge. "We should have ridden back across it."

"I think you would've had to carry me. My legs feel like rubber."

"I'd carry you," he said.

She laughed. "It's a long way. Even for a soldier."

He laughed, too. "You're right. But for you, I'd do it."

She felt safe with Grayson. She believed that he really would carry her if he needed to. It was almost like her heart had been on hold – waiting for him to come back. Why hadn't she known that? Why hadn't she looked for him?

Life. Life was the answer. Life always moved forward.

But once in a lifetime, the lucky ones got a chance to start over and do the important things again.

She was one of the lucky ones. And Grayson was one of the important things.

She squeezed his hand.

He smiled into her eyes. "I love you," he said.

"I love you, too," she said.

As the ferry took off across the water, the wind racing in her face, she didn't know if the tears were from the wind or from the rare moment of blissful happiness.

The water was choppy, but Grayson put his arm around her and held her close.

"Let's take a picture," he said, taking out his camera and holding it out at arm's length. Leaning their heads together, they smiled for the camera. Then smiled at each other. Grayson snapped the pictures.

As they looked at the images, Claire said, "I think you should take them over. Maybe later after we've had a shower."

He laughed. "We can take some more." But he didn't delete and she was too tired to care.

It was an ordeal getting their bicycles – Claire had never seen that many bikes piled together in one place. She'd stood back and let Grayson find them among the throngs of people searching for their own bicycles.

They rode them back to the bike shop and turned them in. Then they had to walk back to the SUV before they could finally drive to the hotel.

Claire got into the shower and let the hot water run over

her exhausted muscles. How could she feel so spent and so content at the same time?

She dried her hair with the blow dryer and waited while Grayson showered.

While she waited she lay on the bed – for just a moment and that's when her legs really began to ache.

When Grayson came out, she said, "I don't like to complain, but my legs hurt. I mean it hurts like a toothache."

"Here," he said, taking pillows and putting them beneath her legs. He went to his toiletry bag and brought her two aspirin and a bottle of water. "Take these."

He sat down beside her as she took the medication.

"You don't hurt?" she asked.

"No," he said, "but remember I have the advantage. Years of P.T."

"I'd never make it," she said.

"You'd be surprised. So tomorrow, we'll do it all over again."

"You've gone insane."

"Maybe a little. Did that help?" He asked, gesturing to the pillows.

"No," she said.

"Maybe I can help," he said.

He started with her feet and massaged his way up to her calves. "Is this where it hurts?"

CLAIRE MUMBLED something that he took to be a yes. He knew this kind of pain, though it had been a long time. He'd be sore tomorrow, but sore was preferable to this deep muscle pain that she was experiencing.

Her skin was smooth as silk and when he glanced at her face, her eyes were closed in sensations of bliss.

He could seduce her now. He had no doubt about that.

But he wouldn't do that.

He'd done that once. Twenty years ago and the regret still ate at him. He never should have seduced her the night before he'd been shipping out for basic training. But they'd been kids and it was how they'd shown their love for each other. It was how they'd been trying to bind themselves together.

But not this time. This time he knew they would see each other again soon, but he wasn't willing to take the chance that history could repeat itself.

He loved her too much to risk hurting her again.

Her phone buzzed. He reached over, picked up her phone from the nightstand, and held it out for her. She cracked one eye open.

"It's text," he said.

"Danielle?"

He glanced at her phone. "I don't think so."

"You check it. I'm too tired.

He read the message. *Hi Claire. Did you read my proposal? Let me know what you think and I can schedule a visit.*

"It's from someone named Allen."

"What does he want?" She muttered against the pillow.

"He wants to come visit."

"Later," she said. He chuckled, but there was more to this story that he would have to find out later when she wasn't drunk with sleep. He set the phone aside, his brow furrowed with worry.

As he massaged her calves, she fell asleep. He climbed into bed and, pulling her into his arms, slept next to her.

15

---

laire sat outside Dr. Lee's office and waited while Claire had her therapy session. It was Tuesday and she was thinking about tonight. Grayson was planning to leave Thursday morning. That gave them two more nights together before he left. They had talked about it and after their trip to San Francisco, they both wanted to just stay home and enjoy the quietness of each other's company.

To distract herself, she was reading a novel by Isabella Quinn called Forgotten. Lost in the fictional world, she didn't see the door open and Danielle come out.

"Mom?" Danielle said. "Dr. Lee wants you to come in."

Claire closed her iPad as fear shot through her. "Is everything okay?" she asked as she gathered up her handbag. She thought Danielle was doing so well. She knew that Danielle's relationship with Joey had cooled, but Danielle always had boyfriends who came and went. Her issue had never been related to that.

"I'll wait out here," Danielle said as Claire hurried into Dr. Lee's office.

"Claire," he said. "Sit down."

"Is something wrong with Danielle?" she asked.

"No, no. Danielle is doing quite well," he said. "It's you I want to talk about."

"Me? Why?"

"Danielle tells me your boyfriend is moving away soon."

"Thursday," she said.

"This is the same man who abandoned you in high school."

"He didn't abandon me exactly."

"No, I understand," he said. "It was all a misunderstanding. But it felt like abandonment." He paused a moment. "For over twenty years."

Claire took a deep breath.

Dr. Lee was right, of course. "We probably shouldn't be talking about me," she said.

"I know. It's hard to talk about yourself."

Claire laughed and shifted in her chair. She'd come here for Danielle. Now Dr. Lee was wanting to delve into her brain.

"I'm okay," she said.

"I'm sure you are" he agreed. "I'm just wondering how you're coping with all this."

She pressed her hands together. "We're still going to see each other."

He nodded.

"I know. We planned to see each other last time, too, but we were kids. We weren't in control of things that happened."

"You feel in control now," he said.

Claire shifted again. "No. Not really."

"But you're okay with him leaving."

"I'm not okay with it. I just don't have a choice."

Dr. Lee nodded again. And waited. "You're very brave," he said.

"I'm not brave," she said.

"You seem brave to me."

"Do I?" she asked with a little laugh. "Because I'm not brave at all."

"You do a good job of hiding your fear."

She nodded. "I was trained to not show emotion."

"That can be a good quality to have at times."

"And not at others. I know."

Dr. Lee sat quietly studying her. "Is there anything you'd like to discuss with me?"

Claire shook her head. "No, but I appreciate your concern."

"Can I give you some unsolicited advice?"

"Of course."

"Don't keep it all bottled inside. Find a way to let yourself feel. Not all the time, just during a time that you choose. When you're alone. I think you'll find that you can cope much better if you let yourself feel emotions from time to time."

Claire nodded. "I do. I do feel emotions with Grayson."

"That's good." Dr. Lee took his glasses off. Claire had watched him enough with Danielle to know that it was a sign he had something significant he was about to say. "Have you found that you've been able to forgive him?"

"Yes," she said.

"But do you sometimes have lingering doubts that maybe history is replaying itself all over again?"

"Yes," she said. How had he known that? She hadn't told anyone.

"That's a difficult thing to get past."

"It is. But it's possible." Claire wasn't sure if she was telling him or asking him.

"It takes a lot of faith and a lot of strength. I admire you for being able to start over with someone who hurt you so much."

"He didn't hurt me on purpose."

Dr. Lee smiled. "Again, I admire you for being willing to give Grayson a second chance. He's a very lucky man. And I think I can safely say that Danielle likes him. She thinks he'd make a great stepfather."

Claire laughed nervously. "That might be a little difficult living so far apart."

Dr. Lee just nodded.

AFTER CLAIRE LEFT Dr. Lee's office, she turned to Danielle. "You told Dr. Lee about me and Grayson."

"I tell him everything."

"I see."

"He's really easy to talk to," Danielle said.

"Uh huh."

"I guess you have to get used to somebody getting into your business."

"I think you're right," Claire admitted as they walked together down the hallway toward the door to the parking lot. "You know, I never told you, Danielle, but I really admire you for how you've opened yourself up this past year and let people help you get past those feelings of hopelessness that you were feeling."

Danielle grinned. "Thanks. I admire you, too."

"Why?" Claire asked.

"Why? For everything. You're so successful. And you let Grayson come back into your life without even a hitch. I think that means you really love him."

"I do love him," she said, the admission warming her heart. Other than Grayson, she hadn't told anyone else. Not even Danielle.

"No," Danielle said, as they climbed into the car and closed the door. "I mean you must REALLY love him."

Claire smiled. "I do." Then she grew serious. "Does that bother you? I mean… Daddy."

"Are you kidding? If you and Grayson get married, that means I would have the two most awesome dads ever."

. . .

CLAIRE SAT QUIETLY on her sofa, reading her novel as she waited for Grayson. She'd gotten used to their routine – dinner together every night. They didn't even talk about it anymore. It was just understood. Instead, they talked about where they would eat or what they would cook. What they would watch on TV – a series like *Game of Thrones* or a movie.

Sometimes they just sat quietly and read.

It was going to be lonely without him here in the evenings.

When the doorbell rang, she went to answer it. He was earlier than usual.

When she opened the door and saw him standing there, leaning against the post, with one hand behind his back, her heart melted.

She held out her hand.

"What?" he asked.

She smiled, but kept her hand out.

He reached out and took her hand in his.

She laughed and reached behind his back, but he twisted away and laughed with her.

"I know you have it. I have eleven in the vase. So tonight makes twelve."

"Uh oh," he said, feigning horror. "I knew I was forgetting something."

She reached behind him again, but this time, he let her grab the rose that she had known would be there.

"You've spoiled me," she said.

"You think so?"

"Yes."

"You haven't seen anything yet."

"Is that so?" She took the rose inside and added it to the vase on the kitchen table. There were twelve now. He'd started bringing her one every night, excluding the time they'd spent in San Francisco. He'd even managed to make it work with them being out for two nights. It occurred to her that he must have been planning that trip longer than he'd let on.

Maybe he wasn't as spontaneous as he led her to believe.

She turned and he was standing behind her. He swept her into a hug. She put her arms around him and her fingers dug into his shirt.

He backed away to study her face. "Are you still sore?" he asked.

"No," she said. "But I'm thinking maybe I need to add cycling to my workout. So I'll be ready next time for whatever you come up with. Marathons. Bike rides."

"You never know," he said.

"Nope. I never know." She settled her head back against his chest and told herself he wasn't gone yet. "So how far in advance do you plan these activities?"

"That, my lovely, is a secret I'll never reveal."

"Ah. Secretive and mysterious."

"You'll never be bored with me around," he said, nuzzling at her ear. "What do you want to eat?" he asked.

"I thought we'd make a fried green tomato po'boy."

He laughed. "That's different."

"I have them all the time for lunch with Danielle." She bit her lip. "I've never made one though."

"Do you have all the ingredients?"

"I'm always prepared," she said.

"Okay," he said, taking her hand and pulling her with him to the kitchen. "I'm starving."

She laughed. "You're always starving."

"It's true. You've found me out."

LATER THAT EVENING, Claire and Grayson were curled together on the couch like a couple of kittens. Charlie was there with them, coaxing Grayson to rub under his chin. He was getting bigger and Claire pointed out how big his little paws were getting.

"So…" Grayson said, "I don't think you ever answered me."

"Hmm. About what?"

"About having another child."

"That's not something that can be easily answered."

"Danielle told me that Noah's wife is expecting. You two are about the same age, aren't you? And it's her first."

"I think she might be a little older. And, yes, Danielle told me that, too."

"Well?"

"Our situations are different."

"You're so avoiding answering me," he said, kissing her earlobe.

"Oh no. You're leaving tomorrow."

"What?" he asked innocently.

"We are so not going down that road again."

"Don't worry. When I ravish you, I don't plan for us to leave the bed for a week."

"A week, huh?"

"Yep. I just can't decide between a cruise or holing up in a mountain cabin."

"The cabin sounds nice. But it sounds like we're gonna need room service. Besides, I've already done the whole honeymoon cruise thing. It's overrated."

"See there, I have you already planning our honeymoon."

"You're kinda sneaky, aren't you? I didn't know you were such a planner."

"You have no idea how much work goes into being spontaneous," he said.

"You're right. It's much easier to plan things."

"Are you sure I can't talk you into driving with me? We can stop off at the Grand Canyon and spend a couple of nights."

"I thought you didn't allow time for sight-seeing."

"For you, I would be late."

"Not a chance," she said. "You'll be fired before you even get there."

"I've got until Monday."

"You know I would, but I've got that fundraiser Saturday. It's been planned for months."

"And you've only known me for weeks," he said.

"Yet somehow it seems like years," she said.

They laughed, then sat quietly with the television playing a movie neither of them were watching.

"So, I'm thinking I'll call you every night," he said.

"Okay."

GRAYSON DIDN'T WANT to leave. Once he walked out that the door, he ran the risk of destroying the fairytale life they'd created.

A year – even nine months – until next May was a long time.

So much could go wrong.

He may not be able to find a job back in L.A. He could live off his retirement from the military, but Claire would expect more out of him. He needed to have another career.

To be successful and make her proud.

Besides, he'd seen too many good men crash and burn after retirement. It was crucial for a man to keep working. He couldn't risk ending up psychologically disabled.

But he had to leave. He had a long day of driving tomorrow.

He held her close. He would be back.

It's a temporary separation.

He needed to believe that.

A long-distance relationship was one thing. A long-distance marriage was another thing entirely.

I'll make it work.

He had to believe it.

"You should go," she said, sitting up.

"I don't want to."

"Good. I don't want you to either." She stood up and tugged on his arm. "Come on."

"I should have known you'd kick me out eventually."

"It had to happen."

"Come on," she said again, "I'll walk you to the door."

At the door, they held on to each other as the seconds ticked past.

Until she nudged him again. "Go," she said. "You need to be well rested. I don't want to be the reason you fall asleep at the wheel."

He kissed her softly. "I'll see you soon," he said. "my love."

Her eyes were closed. Charlie meowed and stood up to put his front paws on Grayson's jeans.

"He's saying good-bye, too," Claire said, picking up her kitten and holding him to her.

"Be safe," she said.

Grayson turned and went out the front door. His eyes stung from unshed tears.

This was one of those things in life that felt so very wrong.

He'd set a course for himself that he longer wanted to follow. But he had no choice. He had to honor his commitment.

A soldier followed through.

He listened until he heard the door lock and her alarm beep into place.

Then he went down the sidewalk, got into his car, and backed out of her driveway.

His heart ached. He needed to get this over with so he could get back to her.

----

16

*C*laire went to the kitchen and, after feeding Charlie, sat at the little table and slid the vase with the roses toward her. A couple of the roses were already dead.

Soon, they would all be dead.

But she would keep them, she decided.

She would keep them because they represented so much planning and thought that Grayson had gone through for her. A rose a day for two weeks giving her a dozen roses.

They represented the love that he had shown for her this summer.

She could only hope and pray that they hadn't gone from high school sweethearts to a summer romance.

She wiped at the tears at her eyes before they could fall from her lashes and pushed the roses back to the center of the table.

She had to trust that whatever was supposed to happen would. She got up and headed upstairs, Charlie scampering at her heels.

Time only moved forward.

. . .

CLAIRE WOKE at her usual time. She'd left the curtains open in her bedroom so the soft morning sunlight was streaming across her face.

She stretched. Everything was as it should be. Danielle had come home late, but was tucked safely in her bed. Claire knew because she'd waited up. Danielle thought she'd gotten lost in the novel she was reading on her iPad, but in truth as soon as Danielle stuck her head in the door to say goodnight, Claire had been out.

But as her brain came more awake, she knew that everything wasn't as it should be. Grayson had left last night. And although they had ended their early evening with kisses and promises to stay in touch, it was going to be different. They'd seen each other every single day for the last few weeks. Now they would merely have phone calls and perhaps at most, monthly visits.

Claire couldn't help comparing this separation with the one twenty years ago. They'd been kids then. She wasn't even out of high school. They'd had sex their last night together before he shipped out. Sex for the first time.

This time they hadn't had sex, but they had been attached at the hip.

They'd been more physically intimate last time and more emotionally intimate this time.

Claire climbed out of bed and got into the shower. She did her best thinking in the shower, but not today. Today she was unable to sort through the emotional tangles in her head.

Today was the first day of trying to get her life back to normal.

She'd known going in that Grayson would be leaving. Knowing that had made their time together bittersweet. She wasn't the teenager anymore. The one who believed that anything was possible.

She knew that them having careers on opposite sides of the

country wasn't going to work out. Relationships couldn't work that way. Sure, it would be exciting for a little while to visit and see each other. She'd go to Pittsburgh and see some snow.

But if anyone knew how hard it was to stay connected in a long-distance relationship, it was Claire. She'd lived with Noah, her ex-husband, but he'd been away from home more than he'd been there. Even if she'd wanted to have something deeper with him, it would've been next to impossible with that physical distance.

Time moves in only direction. Focus on the future.

She got dressed for a meeting with her board of directors. Woke Danielle to say good-bye before she left home. Stopped on her way to work for a latte at Starbuck's.

Kept her attention on the moment.

Halfway through her meeting, her phone buzzed with a text from Grayson.

I miss you. I hope your meeting is going well.

How much longer would he know her schedule?

It wouldn't be long. He'd get caught up in his own world. The excitement of his new job.

She shook off the feelings of negativity.

Day by day.

That's how she'd get through it

It's how she'd gotten through it last time he'd left and it was how she'd gotten through her marriage with Noah. Then her divorce.

One day at the time.

She picked up Danielle and they went to the York and Orleans for lunch.

"What's wrong, Mom?" Danielle asked, minutes after they had sat at their table.

"Nothing," she said.

"It's okay to miss Grayson," she said. "I miss him, too."

Claire forced a smile on her lips. "We'll see him soon," she said.

"Of course, we will," Danielle agreed.

Claire asked Danielle about her upcoming orientation for Fall classes and listening allowed her to sit quietly and focus on her daughter.

That night Danielle spent the night at the university for orientation, so Claire had the house to herself for the first time in a long time.

The timing probably wasn't the best. It allowed Claire time alone to think. A mixed blessing.

She sat on the sofa with Charlie nestled close to her and looked through the photo album from twenty years ago. She'd been a teenager when she'd put it together, but now the same feelings were back. The same feelings she'd felt the last time Grayson left.

She closed the photo album and opened the photos on her phone. Smiled at the pictures of the two them interspersed with pictures of the three of them. Claire and Grayson. And Danielle.

It was the same. Yet different.

Her phone rang and Grayson's picture appeared on her screen, jarring her out of her thoughts.

"Hey, where are you?" she asked.

"Albuquerque, New Mexico."

"Really? Wow. I thought you might want to stop and see the Grand Canyon."

"No. I couldn't do that. I'll wait until I'm with you."

"Grayson…" she said.

"I miss you."

She squeezed her eyes closed tightly. "I miss you, too."

It was the same. Why was it so different?

"Grayson," she said again.

"What is it Claire?"

"What were we thinking?"

"We were thinking that we have something special and we can make it work."

Silence.

"Claire?"

"Yes?"

"Have you met someone else already? Is it that Maine D'Court guy? Is he there?"

Claire laughed and felt better than she had felt all day.

"Please say no," he said.

"No," she said, a tear slipping down her cheek. "What about Allen?"

"Who?"

"Allen. The guy who's coming for a visit."

She laughed. "I turned down his proposal."

"Promise?"

"I promise."

"Good. We're good then."

When they hung up the phone, Claire hugged her cat to her and cried into his fur. "I don't think I can do it, Charlie," she said and rubbed the tears from his fur. Once Grayson arrived safely in Pittsburgh, she would tell him. She would tell him she couldn't do this whole long distance relationship thing.

GRAYSON GOT UP EARLY the next morning and like every morning, the first thing he did was check his phone. His screen saver was Claire's picture. He opened up his phone and scrolled to his photos. Holding his finger against his favorite photo to animate it, he watched the two of them smile and kiss on the ferry with the Golden Gate Bridge behind them. He'd never seen her look so beautiful as she did in that wind-swept exhausted moment. Her defenses had been down and the love she felt for him was in her face.

He put his suitcase in his car, and filled up his tank with gas. The further away he got from Los Angeles and Claire, the more anxious he became. He had an odd sensation that the tie that bound them would break if he got too far away. Pennsylvania seemed like such a long way away. Maybe he should have sold his car and flown. If he'd flown, he'd be there by now and he wouldn't be dealing with the prolonged sensation of getting further and further away from her.

Within the hour, he was struggling to see the road in front of him. The morning sunlight in the desert was blinding. It took all his concentration to keep his car on his side of the highway.

He decided to stop at a waffle house for breakfast to take a break. Perhaps if he took a break, the sun would shift and it would be less hazardous to drive.

As he waited for his eggs and bacon to arrive, he turned off his cell phone and turned it back on. His service had been spotty since he'd hit New Mexico.

He had a phone message from yesterday.

He played the message as his food arrived. Then played it again.

His face broke out into a wide grin.

And the weight of the world fell off his shoulders.

It was already nine o'clock in Pittsburgh. He quickly ate his breakfast, then replayed the message.

He then called the department chair in Pittsburgh who had hired him.

After a few minutes of conversation, he realized that he'd just made someone else's day.

He needed to make another phone call, but he had to wait two hours. He got back in the car and this time, the sun was at his back. He turned on his music and sang along to a James Taylor song.

. . .

THAT EVENING, Claire worked late. When she finally got home, she was too exhausted to worry much about dinner. She sent out for Chinese and turned on the TV while she waited. Everything was on autopilot for her next fundraiser. It had been a very productive week. She had nothing pressing to do at the moment.

She needed something to keep herself from thinking. She dragged herself off the couch and began putting clothes in the washer. It was time to do some cleaning.

The Chinese place usually took about an hour because it was a little bit of a drive for the delivery guy. But Claire always gave him a big tip, so he didn't mind driving out her way.

She hadn't been watching the clock, but when the doorbell rang, she instinctively knew it was about time for the delivery guy to arrive.

She went to the door and opened it without peeking outside first.

No one was standing there. Pulling the door to behind her to keep Charlie from following, she looked left, then right.

Grayson must have been pacing on her porch. He was walking toward her.

"Now what if I'd been a serial killer," he said, stopping a few feet in front of her.

"Grayson?" Her mind struggled to link the pieces together.

She hadn't heard from him all day, but last night he'd been in New Mexico. On his way east. To Pittsburgh.

Now he was standing here on her doorstep.

Perhaps she was imagining things.

While her brain was in lockdown, he took two steps and pulled her into his arms, sweeping her feet off the ground.

He twirled her around, then set her down.

Her blood was flowing again.

"What are you doing here?" she asked. "You're supposed to be heading the other direction."

"I love you, Claire."

Her heart skittered and she smiled. "I love you, too." She waited a heartbeat. "Is your phone broken?"

He laughed. "Nope. But my heart was breaking."

"I don't understand. You came all this way just to tell me that. Are you going to be late?"

"Nope. Not taking the job."

She stared at him. Her brain trying to make sense of it all. She rubbed her palm against the side of her head. "Wait. You said you had to take this job. You couldn't let down the university in Pittsburgh."

"Maybe it was something about driving alone through the desert for hours, but I had an epiphany."

"What kind of epiphany?" she asked, not bothering to keep the skepticism out of her voice.

"I'm not the only person who needs a job right now. There's a whole line of people who'd like that job in Pittsburgh."

"I'm sure. But…"

The Chinese delivery guy drove up to the curb.

"Are you expecting someone?" Grayson asked.

"Yes," she said, keeping a straight face.

"I see." He took a step back.

Claire was a little surprised at the pain on his features until she realized he thought the delivery guy was another guy coming over.

"Grayson," she said.

He shook his head. "It's okay. I shouldn't have assumed."

"Grayson," she laughed.

"Here's your delivery, ma'am."

"Thank you, Robert," she said, signing the receipt and adding her tip.

"Have a great evening," Robert said, heading back toward his car.

Grayson just watched her.

"Come inside," she said.

"I'm a little tired," he said.

"It's okay. Come in. Eat some Chinese food with me. And tell me how you ended up back here."

He smiled. "I hit the wrong button on my GPS."

"Ha." They settled into the living room and opened the boxes of food. "What happened with the teaching job? Did they cancel or something?"

"No. I canceled on them."

"But you said."

"I know. I had a sense of obligation, but after I called the department chair, she assured me that they had a list of people waiting. They had given me preference because I'm a veteran."

"Out of a list of equally qualified people."

"Exactly."

"You turned down the job?"

He nodded.

"Help me understand."

"First I need to ask you something."

"Okay."

"Do you think I could borrow your guest room for awhile?"

"Of course. While you look for another job?"

"I already have another job."

"Oh." Her heart sank. He wasn't going to Pennsylvania, but he would be going somewhere else instead. She set down her fork with a sudden loss of appetite. She'd been so happy to see him, she hadn't realized that he must going to take the full-time position in Texas. What was it about Texas and her men anyway? Noah had been from Texas. He was living in Alabama now, but he still had a business based out of Fort Worth. Now Grayson was going to be living in Texas. Where was it? San Antonio? It didn't matter. It was Texas and not here.

"Claire," he said. "I'm staying here."

She shook her head. Grayson wasn't inclined to be

unemployed while he looked for a job. She couldn't allow him to do that. Even if it meant he had to move to Texas.

"I can't let you be unemployed," she said it out loud. "Even if it means moving to Texas."

"They already filled the position in Texas."

"You can't not work," she said.

"Claire," he said again. "Look at me."

She looked up. Met his gaze. Took a deep breath.

"I'm going to work for the VA."

The VA. He'd said that was a possibility for the future. That it was really hard to get a job there. "But…"

"I know. I said they wouldn't hire me because they rarely have openings. But they did."

"They hired you?"

He nodded.

"Here? In L.A.?"

"Yep."

"For good. Permanently?"

"Yes," he said. "I got really, really lucky."

"This is like… a miracle."

"Fate is keeping us together this time."

"Wow," she said. Then she threw her arms around him. He pulled her into his lap and held her tightly to him.

"There's nothing keeping us apart anymore," he said. "Except maybe the Chinese delivery guy."

Claire started laughing. Then she couldn't stop. "I can't believe you thought I'd have a guy over already," she said through giggles.

"I don't ever have to worry about that again." He waited a beat. "Right?"

"You don't have to."

"Claire," he nudged her back to look into her eyes. "I know how much you love this house."

She nodded. She didn't want to leave here.

"That means you'll have to invite me to stay here with you."

"I'll think about it," she said.

His expression sobered. "It'll be awkward if you don't want your husband to live here with you."

"I don't have a husb…" She stopped talking and stared into his eyes. "Anymore…"

"Do you think you could tolerate another one?"

"I'll think about it," she said, swallowing the lump in her throat. She was overcome with emotion. Emotion that threatened to spill over and consume her.

"One who's around all the time, especially in the evenings and weekends."

"I don't know," she said, biting her lip to keep her face from splitting into a ridiculous grin.

"Think hard," he said. "Because you're about to have to make that decision."

"What do you mean?"

"I like you, so I'll warn you. You're about to be proposed to." He dumped her off his lap onto the sofa and before she knew what he was doing, he was kneeling on the floor. "Claire Beauchamp…" he said. "Worthington…." He started over. "Claire… Will you marry me?"

She couldn't hold it any longer. Her face split into that ridiculous grin. "Yes!" She slid onto the floor with him.

He pulled her against him and they ended up lying side by side on the floor, arms wrapped around each other.

He swept the hair from her face and lifted her hand. Kissed her knuckles. "Tomorrow," he murmured. "Tomorrow we'll go shopping and get something to put on this finger." He kissed her ring finger and she thought her heart might burst with happiness.

Then he was kissing her. Suddenly he stopped and looked into her eyes.

"Will Danielle be back tomorrow?" he asked.

"Yeah. Why?"

"I was thinking we could find a Justice of the Peace tomorrow."

Her eyes widened. "Tomorrow?"

"I don't want you to have a chance to get away this time. Besides, I don't have anywhere to live, so I need to lock this thing down."

"You're such a romantic," she said.

He grinned. "Let me show you just how romantic."

Then his lips were on hers again.

Claire's befuddled mind worked to make sense of all that was happening. Grayson was back. For good. And tomorrow she would be his wife. Then her emotions trumped her thoughts.

And she was lost in his kiss.

No matter how they got here.

Life moved in only one direction. Forward.

How about a free short story?

GET MY BONUS SHORT STORY
https://BookHip.com/VDSLNKM

ARE you ready for Danielle's story? Read the next sweet story in the For the Love of the Flight Series.

Turn the page for a preview of FALLING AGAIN…

PREVIEW FALLING AGAIN

CHAPTER 1

*A*t the moment, Danielle Worthington was having a hard time believing in true love, much less happily ever after.

After unclipping the camera from the tripod, she adjusted the camera's shutter speed and photographed the models in front of her. The models were *posing* as a happy couple. They wore jeans and t-shirts to portray a casual, relaxed look, and stood in front of an historic wooden house with a white picket fence at Sam Houston Park.

They were depicting the American Dream.

Their smiles looked true and their affection genuine, but Avery and Jacob could barely stand the sight of each other.

Jacob put his arm around Avery and pulled her close. They gazed at each other, their faces only inches apart. Danielle went up the stairs and stood on the other side of them. She took more photos. They were such a cute couple.

"I've got enough casual," Danielle said. "Go get dressed up, guys."

As Jacob and Avery turned away from each other, their

smiles turned to scowls. At least they were professional enough to pretend to like each other during the shoots.

Danielle glanced at her phone. She had two hours to get back to her office in time to meet her father for lunch. A wave of anxiety swept over her in anticipation of that meeting.

She took a deep breath and swallowed the nausea. Her father loved her no matter what. *Right?*

He'd always been there for her. There was no reason why he wouldn't be there for her now.

Avery and Jacob were back within minutes. Avery was now wearing a red party dress, and Jacob was wearing a black tux.

They made such a beautiful couple.

Danielle's heart did a little summersault as an image of *that* night flashed through her mind. The night that she had worn a floor-length red dress, and Joey had worn a black suit. Danielle had felt like a princess that night. She'd thought they were in a fairy tale.

The fairy tale hadn't collapsed at midnight, but at six a.m. the next morning. That girl, whatever her name was, had been surprised that Joey wasn't alone. In fact, that was the only satisfaction that Danielle took from the whole fiasco.

Now she saw her relationship with Joey for what it had been all along: a sham, just like Avery and Jacob. She'd fallen for an illusion.

Never again.

After taking several more photos, she could tell that they were getting tired, and she needed to rest too.

Walking back to the parking lot, she enjoyed the warmth of the Houston sun. She'd lived here for six weeks now, but already she had found that she liked the friendliness of the people and the warmth of the weather.

A Los Angeles native, Houston wouldn't have been her first choice. She had an affinity for New York, though she'd only visited there once with her stepmother, Savannah, whose love for the big city had been contagious.

Nonetheless, Danielle was content with Houston.

Except for one small detail.

When she got to the parking lot, she had to call an Uber. Houston was definitely a driving town, and Danielle would be content if she never had to drive.

After the Uber driver picked her up, she noticed an American flag decal on his rearview mirror. Seeing it was like taking an instant punch to the gut.

Her ex-boyfriend, ex of five weeks and four days, was in the Air Force, stationed here in Houston. They'd been on-again-off-again for several years. When he'd suggested she move to Houston, she'd thought they were moving forward. Together.

Unfortunately, she'd been moving forward alone. Danielle had subsequently implemented a self-imposed dating moratorium. It hadn't been hard to do since she was in a strange town and knew absolutely no one other than coworkers. And since they all worked independently, she really didn't know them either.

She'd found a furnished apartment to rent, a job, and left home for the first time.

Okay, she admitted to herself that there were other factors involved. One, her mother had just gotten married a second time, this time to her high school sweetheart, so moving out of the house was long overdue. And second, Houston put her a little closer to her father, who lived in Alabama and had a charter flight company in Fort Worth.

Though she hadn't seen him in nearly two months, he was flying down today to take her to lunch for her birthday. Today, she would tell him that she and Joey had broken up, and she was living alone in Houston. And again, the thought made her queasy. Odd. She'd never been nervous about seeing her father before.

Maybe she'd picked up a virus.

Keep Reading Falling Again…

Kathryn Kaleigh is the author of over seventy novels, over one hundred short stories, and many collections.

kathrynkaleigh.com